"Don't play your sexy games with me,"

Jarrod said hoarsely.

Georgia's lips parted with involuntary provocation and her tongue tip moistened her dry mouth. She lifted her hand to rest it gently along his jaw, moved her fingers to trace the outline of his mouth.

"Leave it, Georgia, for both our sakes. Unless you want to take the consequences."

His words cut through her and the old wounds bled, transporting her agonizingly back in time. She was that naive, trusting, so-in-love nineteen-year-old again. "Don't you want me, Jarrod?"

"Want you? Oh, yes, I want you, Georgia. That's one of the jokes of my life. I'll go on wanting you with every breath...."

LYNSEY STEVENS was born in Brisbane, Queensland, and before beginning to write she was a librarian. It was in secondary school that she decided she wanted to be a writer.

"Writers, I imagined," Lynsey explains, "lived such exciting lives—traveling to exotic places, making lots of money and not having to work. I have traveled. However, the tax man loves me dearly and no one told me about typist's backache and frustrating lost words!" When she's not writing she enjoys reading and cross-stitching and she's interested in genealogy.

Close Relations

LYNSEY STEVENS

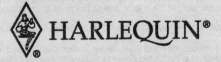

HARLEQUIN®

TORONTO • NEW YORK • LONDON
AMSTERDAM • PARIS • SYDNEY • HAMBURG
STOCKHOLM • ATHENS • TOKYO • MILAN • MADRID
PRAGUE • WARSAW • BUDAPEST • AUCKLAND

ISBN 0-373-80523-3

CLOSE RELATIONS

First North American Publication 1999.

Visit us at www.eHarlequin.com

Printed in U.S.A.

CHAPTER ONE

JARROD took the new exit off the main Brisbane to Ipswich highway and approached the roundabout. There weren't many people about but he remembered that at certain times of the day this area could become chock-a-block with local traffic.

The small shopping centre had mushroomed in the four years he'd been away and he grimaced. It was hardly the sleepy little town it had been when his father had first brought him here when he had been a troubled thirteen-year-old.

He accelerated out of the turn and took the right fork past the Honour Stone. On his right was the small group of businesses that used to constitute the sum total of the village's commercial centre. Groceries. Fruit shop. Drapery. Bank.

A car shot out of the parking area in front of the shops and sped up the hill. That much hadn't changed. Disaster Alley they'd half-jokingly called it. One car tried to leave and other shoppers vied aggressively for the vacant parking space.

He followed the winding road lined with houses that ranged from the wooden Queenslanders with their wide verandas to the aesthetic angles of architectural designs in brick and tile. Rolling paddocks had now well and truly become sprawling suburbia.

At least the fifty acres around his father's home would still be intact. His father would never sell his land. Apart from the one block he'd sold to his best friend, Geoff Grayson. And his wife. Why wouldn't his father want Geoff Grayson's wife nearby? he asked himself bitterly.

Pushing a surge of painful memories out of his mind, he

increased the speed of the car, for the first time wanting to see the large old house that had been home to him for his adolescence. And that need overcame his reluctance to revisit his father and stepmother—the family he had turned his back on four years ago.

His father. He'd never managed to call Peter Maclean that. And yet Peter Maclean was his biological father. A mere accident of conception, one of nature's jokes, he reflected wryly, without bitterness.

He'd learned the truth about his parentage just before his mother died of cancer. She'd told him of the brief affair she'd had with the handsome Queenslander. Peter Maclean had been visiting Western Australia as a consulting engineer and his mother had been the temporary secretary assigned to him.

Three weeks later Peter Maclean had left for home, unaware that the young woman he'd spent most of his time with in Perth was pregnant. His mother had had no inclination to contact his father and had decided to raise her son alone.

And she'd done her best to do so. When he'd questioned his mother about his absent father she had told him his father was dead, killed in a construction-site accident before he was born.

The construction-site accident had been partially true, he'd learned later. The accident had happened after he was born but his father had not been killed: Peter Maclean had returned to the west some years later only to be very badly injured when a mobile crane collapsed on a building he was working on.

At first he'd been blazingly angry when his mother had told him the truth—that his father was alive. He'd been angry with everyone, especially with his mother for lying to him and for getting ill. And he'd been angry with the man he'd seen as shirking his responsibilities.

His anger had driven him to reckless behaviour. He'd played truant, become wild and uncontrollable, and he'd had a run-in with the local police. It had been the local police sergeant who had contacted his father when his mother had died.

In retrospect he had to admire Peter Maclean. It must have come as something of a shock to discover he'd got a teenage son, let alone to have the boy foisted on him out of the blue. But Peter had flown immediately to Perth and had spent a couple of weeks getting to know his son before bringing him home.

Home. He sighed. Strangely, all those years ago it *had* felt like coming home.

Home. Where the heart is. Where his heart was broken. His lips twisted self-derisively. He was being rather fanciful, wasn't he? Yet deep inside him he knew he'd left his heart here. He also told himself that if it hadn't been for his father's declining health he wouldn't be returning. But his father was gravely ill and he owed him this visit, this accepting of the olive branch extended to the prodigal son.

Home. Yes, for all that it was worth, he was coming home.

Home. Georgia Grayson sighed as her workmate turned her car and pulled up on the gravel verge in front of the weathered old house. Home at last.

She specially appreciated the lift tonight because she felt so exhausted, as though the weight of the world was resting on her shoulders. Usually when she was at work in the bookshop Georgia could put any troubles on hold, but not at the moment. She had too much on her mind—that was the problem. Everything seemed to have happened at once.

Until recently her life had been drifting along just the way she liked it to be—well ordered, no highs, no lows. Now all that had changed.

That change had begun two weeks ago, when her father had gone up the coast, taking on a house-renovation job that would keep him away for anything up to a couple of months. Then her parked car had been extensively damaged by a runaway truck, leaving her without transport.

On top of that her young sister had announced she was leaving home to share a flat with her boyfriend. Morgan was only seventeen and unemployed and Georgia had tried valiantly to dissuade her, to convince her she was making a mistake.

But last week the thing she had feared most had occurred. Uncle Peter Maclean had had another massive heart attack and his condition was grave. It was only the old man's iron will that had kept him alive this long. Now even that strong will was fading.

So his only son had come home. After four long years. And she knew he'd been back for nearly a week.

Pain twisted inside Georgia, clutching at her heart. Miraculously she'd managed to be out on the two occasions he had called at their house but she knew she wouldn't be able to avoid him for much longer. He was, after all, their cousin. Well, their step-cousin.

'Thanks for dropping me home, Jodie,' she said as she opened the door of her workmate's car. 'Saves me the twenty-minute train trip and then a taxi ride to the house.'

'No worries.' Jodie grinned in the dim interior light. 'It was rotten luck about your car.'

'Could have been worse, I guess. I could have been in it at the time.' Georgia smiled wryly. 'But the insurance company assures me it will all be settled in a couple of weeks.' She rolled her eyes. 'Famous last words. If you can believe them. I didn't realise how much I depended on the car. Living out here off the bus route has decided disadvantages, that's for sure.'

'Well, I don't mind giving you a lift when we're on the same shift.' Jodie glanced over at the lighted house. 'Looks like your brother's home,' she said casually, and Georgia suppressed a smile.

Jodie was a little smitten by Georgia's brother and had been very disappointed to discover that Lochlan was already engaged.

'Did he tell you we went along to see his band play the other night?'

'Yes. He said he'd seen you.' Georgia gathered up her bag.

'The band's really hot. I think they're going places. Lockie said they'd been asked to return to the venue for another stint in a month or so.'

'Yes. He was pleased.' Georgia climbed out of the car. 'See you tomorrow. And thanks again, Jodie.' She closed the door and Jodie drove away.

With a sigh Georgia pushed open the gate. What females saw in her brother she didn't know. It was true that Lockie was quite nice-looking, and he was a fine musician, but—well, they didn't have to live with him.

The lights in the house were blazing so her brother must be home. She noticed his van wasn't standing in its usual spot in the driveway so he'd probably parked it around the back of the house. Unless he'd gone off and forgotten to lock up again.

Slowly Georgia climbed the steps, the old weathered treads rattling a little loosely on their wooden stringers. The house, a high-set old colonial building with a wide veranda on the front and down one side, badly needed attention, but their father always seemed to be busy working on other people's houses.

She pushed open the lattice door at the top of the stairs and crossed the veranda to step into the hall that ran the length of the house.

'That you, Georgie?' Her brother put his head around the living-room doorway. 'I thought you were going to be late tonight.'

Georgia joined him, tossing her bag onto an old but comfortable lounge chair, unbuttoning the short-sleeved navy jacket that matched the skirt she wore. 'Don't call me Georgie and I *am* late. It's nine-thirty. And I would have been later if Jodie hadn't been kind enough to give me a lift home. Where's Mandy?'

Lockie sighed despondently and Georgia noticed for the first time that her usually exuberant brother was uncharacteristically subdued.

He was six feet tall and wore his fairish hair over-long, and his thin, artistic features made him look the musician he was. And although Lockie was nearly five years older than Georgia's twenty-three years, at times she felt as if things were the other way around, that she was the older of the two.

Amanda Burne, Lockie's fiancée of six months and the lead singer in his band, Country Blues, lived with the Grayson family and had a part-time job as a waitress in a local restaurant.

'I didn't think Mandy was working tonight,' Georgia prompted.

'She wasn't—and as a matter of fact she won't be, it seems.' Lockie grimaced and sank onto the arm of the chair opposite his sister. 'She's gone home.'

Georgia raised her eyebrows. 'To New Zealand?'

'I put her on a plane a couple of hours ago.'

'Lockie, what happened?' Georgia asked him quietly.

'No big deal.' Lockie shrugged. 'Her sister's baby arrived early and she's gone home to help out.'

'Is that all it is?' Georgia asked him. She knew that Lockie and Mandy had been at odds over what Mandy termed 'Lockie's lack of drive'.

'Well, you know how motivated Mandy is.' Lockie stood up and moved restlessly across the room. 'She's sort of used this family event to issue me with a bit of an ultimatum.'

Georgia frowned. 'What sort of an ultimatum? You don't mean she's called off the engagement, do you?'

'No. Not exactly. You know she hasn't been happy about— well, about things lately, and she wants some changes made.'

'By "things" I suppose you mean the band?'

He nodded and Georgia watched him as he continued to prowl about the room.

'Mandy says we've been going nowhere and she's sick and tired of all the two-bit gigs Country Blues has been doing. She wants me to get organised and work out a plan to get the band ahead, otherwise…' He pursed his lips.

'Otherwise?' Georgia encouraged gently.

'Otherwise she's going to leave Country Blues and take up an offer from a group in Sydney. She has a month to decide on the Sydney offer and she's going to make the decision when she comes back from New Zealand in a few weeks' time.'

'And if she takes the job in Sydney?'

'Then I guess we're all washed up. The band because we need a female lead singer, and Mandy and I because—well, just because.' Lockie looked down at his hands.

'Do you want to break your engagement?' Georgia asked him.

Lockie sat down again, his long legs stretched out in front of him. 'What do you think, Georgie? You know how I feel about Mandy. I want to marry her and if I had the money I'd do it tomorrow—you know that.'

'Then for heaven's sake do something about it. You can't just sit back and hope it will all come good, Lockie. I know how Mandy feels too, and I can understand it. You've dragged her around the countryside in that clapped-out old van barely making ends meet. You must see it can't go on for ever.'

'But you have to pay your dues in this business and it's the only business I want to be in. My music is my life.'

'And Mandy knows that, but it doesn't mean she has to forfeit what she wants from life. There has to be some compromise.'

'I guess. And I suppose I was expecting too much of her. I thought perhaps I wasn't ready for marriage but when I tried to imagine my life without Mandy I knew I couldn't give her up. And I don't want to, Georgia.' Lockie looked at her directly.

'So what are you going to do?'

He shrugged. 'I don't know.'

'What about that chance of doing the recording you were talking about last week?'

'With D.J. Delaney and Skyrocket Records? That was all talk, sis. We'd need to be seen and heard to even stand a chance. We can't just front up and say, Here we are. We wouldn't get past the front desk.' He stood up again and crossed to the window. 'We'd have to get an engagement at somewhere like the Country Music Club in Ipswich.' His thin features brightened. 'Now, if we could get to work there it would be a stepping stone to anything—recording, television—who knows?'

'Then try for it, Lockie,' Georgia encouraged, and he gave a short laugh.

'Oh, sure, sis. Just walk in and offer the services of the best popular country band in Oz? They'd say, Country Blues who?'

'Why not?' Georgia could almost laugh at herself. Who was she to be offering such earth-shattering advice? She could barely help herself when she had to. She hurriedly pushed that thought out of her mind with an ease borne of an old habit. 'What alternative do you have, Lockie?'

He shook his head. 'Right. About none, I'd say.' He pulled a face but before he could comment further the phone rang and Georgia leant across to lift the receiver.

'Hello?' she said tiredly.

'Georgia? Thank goodness it's you. Can you come and get me?'

'Morgan!' Georgia could hear the agitation in her young sister's voice. 'What's wrong?'

'Do we have to go into that now? I just want to come home.' Morgan's voice rose. 'Is Lockie there? Can you come in his van?'

'Yes, of course. But why? Where's Steve?'

'He's gone out and I don't want to be here when he gets back. We had a fight.'

'What about?' Georgia raised her hand to massage her temple. The headache that had been threatening all day now really made its presence felt, beginning to pound relentlessly.

'For heaven's sake, Georgia!' Morgan exclaimed shrilly. 'It was just a fight. Can't we leave it at that?' She sighed loudly. 'If you must know, Steve hit me and I'm not staying here another day.'

'Steve what?' Georgia asked in dismay.

'If you don't come and get me, Georgia, I'll start walking.'

'You can't do that at this time of night—' Georgia began.

'Then come and get me.'

'All right. Wait there. We should be down in about thirty minutes. And Morgan—'

'Not now, Georgia,' Morgan broke in. 'I'll explain later. I just want to get away from here, OK? So hurry.' With that the young girl hung up.

'What was all that about?' Lockie came to stand beside Georgia as she replaced the receiver.

'Morgan wants us to go and get her. She wants to come home,' she explained.

'Oh, great. That's all we need.' Lockie threw his hands in the air.

'She said she had a fight with Steve and he hit her.'

'Steve? I don't believe it!' Lockie exclaimed. 'Morgan probably hit him first.'

'Oh, Lockie, please.' Georgia ran a hand over her forehead. 'We'll have to go and get her. I'll lock up while you bring the van around.' She went to pick up her bag.

'The van's not here.'

Georgia stopped. 'Not here?'

Her brother shook his head. 'Andy and Ken have got it. Remember I told you Andy's landlord had complained about his drum-practising? Well, he got another place and they borrowed my van to shift his stuff after I took Mandy out to the airport. I don't know when they'll be back.'

Georgia's stomach churned, her tiredness forgotten. 'Then

we'll have to call a taxi.' She turned back to the phone, mentally tallying up how much money she had left out of her pay.

Lockie put his hand on her arm. 'It's OK, Georgie. We won't need a taxi.'

Georgia raised her eyebrows and he coughed nervously. 'Jarrod's coming over. He can drive us down to collect Morgan.'

Georgia froze. She felt as though she'd been transformed into stone. And then she turned her head slowly to face her brother. 'Why is he...?' Her voice faltered and died.

'Why wouldn't he, Georgia?' Lockie asked quietly, his gaze holding hers. 'He's my best friend and he's just returned from the States.'

Georgia fought gallantly to pull herself together as she continued to gaze at her brother. And it was taking more than a little effort to still her galloping pulse, to dislodge the breath that had caught somewhere in her chest.

'Jarrod hasn't seen you yet,' Lockie continued, 'and when I told him you'd be home after nine-thirty he said he'd drop by.'

'I see.' Georgia took a calming breath. 'And I don't suppose it occurred to you that I might not want to see him.'

'You can't live in the past, sis. Four years is a long time, and besides, you'll have to face him some time.'

Four years ago she'd told him hell would freeze over before she'd want to set eyes on him again.

'He's changed a bit,' Lockie was saying. 'He looks older.' He smiled a little awkwardly. 'I told him he was getting quite long in the tooth.'

At that moment they both heard the sound of a car pulling up on the gravel verge in front of the house.

She couldn't face him! You've had four years to recover from his duplicity, a cruel voice reminded her, and she drew a shallow breath.

'Here he is now.' Lockie stated the obvious and his long

fingers gently squeezed her arm. 'And, as I said, what's past is past. It is, isn't it, Georgia?'

She nodded resignedly. If only that were true. 'I suppose it is,' she agreed. 'And we do have to get Morgan. It's lucky he...Jarrod...' the name almost stuck in her throat '...was coming over,' she finished breathily.

Jarrod. There, she'd said his name. For the first time in four years she'd said his name, the sound of it so foreign...and yet so achingly, so hauntingly well-known.

Well-known? She almost laughed out loud. Well-known in what sense? In every sense, she told herself ruthlessly. How could she forget his name? Or him? Jarrod. Jarrod Peter Maclean. Uncle Peter Maclean's only son.

'Georgia?' Lockie touched her arm again and she blinked, coming back to the present with a jolt.

'Yes. We should go,' she said softly, and moved into the hallway.

'Right.' Lockie sounded relieved and headed towards the open front door as a tall figure was taking the steps two at a time with long-legged ease.

'Hi, Lockie.' He smiled a greeting, unaware of Georgia standing like a statue behind her brother.

She made herself move, face him, and her entire body remained numb for just a few seconds. And then it seemed to take on a life of its own.

Her heartbeats accelerated, sending heated blood rushing through her veins. Her hands wanted to reach out to him, to follow the hard lines of his strong jaw, feel the smoothness of his freshly shaved cheek. And her lips longed to taste his again.

With no little effort she pulled her wayward thoughts away from their traitorous yearnings and made herself meet his gaze.

His blue eyes looked black in the dim light yet Georgia was sure she saw them flicker with the same awareness she knew she felt at the sight of him, and she quelled a moment's heady delight.

'Hello, Georgia,' he said evenly. 'I'm sorry to be calling at this hour but Lockie said you were working late tonight. Until now I've always seemed to miss you.'

'And as it turns out it's lucky you did turn up.' Lockie broke into the heavy atmosphere that seemed to Georgia to be pressing in on them as they stood on the wide veranda. 'Do you think you could run us down to Oxley? We've just had a frantic call from Morgan and she wants us to bring her home.'

'Sure.' Jarrod drew his gaze from Georgia and turned back to Lockie. 'What's the problem?'

'Morgan. She's one big problem—' Lockie began.

'And we'd better be going. I did tell Morgan we'd be there in half an hour.' Georgia took a stiff step forward. 'That is, if you wouldn't mind, Jarrod. We could get a taxi.'

'It's no trouble,' he said easily as he turned to retrace his steps.

They were almost down the wide front steps when Lockie stopped. 'I'd better leave a note on the door for Andy just in case he drops the van back before we return. I won't be a moment.' He returned to the house.

And Georgia could only continue on alone with Jarrod. Down the path. To the car.

CHAPTER TWO

JARROD was using one of the company station wagons, 'Maclean Constructions' emblazoned on the side, and he reached around to open the front passenger door for her.

Georgia's nerve-endings were jangling and her stomach churned. She could barely stand, let alone move to get into the car. So she stood there, and after a tense moment of interminable length Jarrod seemed to relax, leaning back, one arm resting along the top of the door.

'Lockie tells me your father's up the coast. How is he these days?'

'You mean, is he drinking?' The words were out before she could draw them back and she sensed the tightening of Jarrod's lips in the darkness.

'No, I wasn't asking that,' he said levelly. 'Peter told me your father hasn't touched alcohol for years.'

For four years, Georgia wanted to tell him, but she had herself under control again. 'He's keeping fairly well,' she said just as evenly. 'He's working on a house up there, renovating. He probably won't be back for a month or so.'

'Does he get plenty of work?'

Did they really care? Jarrod or his father? They'd certainly got rid of him from Maclean's pretty quickly when he'd started drinking after Georgia's mother had died seven years ago. No, that was unfair; Georgia acknowledged the critical voice inside her. It had been her father's choice after his wife's death to leave the engineering firm owned by his brother-in-law. But neither of the Macleans had tried to stop him.

'He gets enough to keep him going,' she said aloud.

That same tension rose again, surging out of the darkness to engulf them, and Georgia's mouth went suddenly dry. Did he remember the nights they'd spent together, the long talks, the drugging kisses, the way their bodies had moved as one to music only they could hear?

Her senses quivered anew, sending an arrow of pure desire hurtling through her heart. Was Jarrod feeling the same almost overwhelming temptation to reach out to her the way she wanted to reach out to him? Georgia swallowed a low moan before it escaped and she swayed slightly just as Jarrod moved.

His hand came out, fingers encircling the hot flesh of her bare arm. Was he simply steadying her? Or was he—?

'Right.' Lockie's footsteps acted like a douche of cold water and Georgia snatched her arm away as though she had been stung. Her brother joined them and if he noticed anything amiss he made no comment. 'Ready to go?' he asked easily.

Then Georgia was in the front of the wagon with her brother beside her and Jarrod had walked around the front to climb in behind the wheel.

'Shove over a bit, sis.' Lockie wriggled and the seat springs protested. 'If this door opens while we're driving along I'll pop out like a cork from a bottle.'

Georgia felt herself grow hot again as she gave her brother a little more room on the bench seat. She fumbled for the sash of her seat belt and both Jarrod and Lockie tried to help her.

Georgia's nerves tightened until she thought they'd snap and as Jarrod reached out to switch on the ignition she barely disguised her flinch. His arm brushed hers as he shifted the gear lever and Georgia wondered if the other two were as aware as she was of that same heightened tension that swelled inside the car.

There was no way Georgia could make any attempt at conversation right then. She was far too busy trying to justify her capricious reactions to her usually dignified, rational self. At least, she'd thought she now had some composure, some control. But perhaps she'd been wrong.

'I'll need directions once we get to Oxley,' Jarrod said as they turned off their narrow road onto the smoother bitumen surface of the main highway.

'Georgia knows the way,' Lockie said casually. 'And I've just had an idea. Andy's new flat is just off the highway at Darra—we go right past it—so if you drop me off there I can bring my van back and save shuttling back and forth with Andy later.'

'Andy may not have finished with your van,' Georgia managed to say, horrified that Lockie would dare to leave her alone again with Jarrod.

'He should be; he hasn't got that much stuff,' Lockie told her, obviously not receiving the frantic silent messages she was trying to send him. 'I can be home by the time you collect Morgan.'

'Lockie—' Georgia began warningly.

'Sounds sensible to me, Georgia,' Jarrod agreed, and Georgia could only wordlessly concede, seething at her brother's insensitivity.

'Has Morgan been flatting long?' Jarrod asked. 'I just can't imagine her being old enough to be out on her own.'

Lockie shifted uncomfortably, glancing sideways at his sister.

'I'm afraid Morgan didn't exactly leave with the family's blessing,' Georgia explained evenly. 'She's only just seventeen and we thought she was too young to move away from home and into a flat with her boyfriend.'

'I see.' Jarrod pulled into the passing lane, easily overtaking a slower car.

'Morgan's going through a bad patch. She decided to leave school and then she couldn't get a job. She's very—well, wilful at present.' Georgia sighed tiredly.

'And how!' put in Lockie. 'I often wondered if the flat was really Steve's idea or if Morgan organised it all. As incomprehensible as it seems, Steve's head over heels in love with her. That's why I find it hard to believe that he actually hit her. It's so out of character.'

'This fellow hit Morgan?' Jarrod asked with a frown.

'So she told Georgia on the phone,' Lockie replied.

'How old is he? Does he have a job?' Jarrod questioned.

'He's a bit older than Morgan, isn't he, Georgia? I'd say nineteen or twenty. Actually he works for your father as an apprentice something or other. I always thought he was a nice guy, pretty quiet and sensible. Didn't you think so too, sis?'

'He is a nice boy—' Georgia began, wishing her brother wasn't so forthcoming about their family problems.

'Not so nice if he hit a woman,' Jarrod broke in drily. 'Any sort of abuse, physical or mental, is unacceptable.'

'Perhaps there can be worse things,' Georgia remarked softly, bitterly, before she could stop herself. The past was waving shadowy fronds to taunt her, and she could sense the sudden stiffening in the man beside her.

'Not in my book,' Jarrod said firmly. 'An argument needn't come to that.'

'You're not wrong. Wife beaters are cowards in mine. Turn left at the next set of lights, Jarrod.' Lockie pointed out the flats where Andy now lived and his battered kombivan was parked outside, Andy and Ken beside it as they lifted a couple of cardboard cartons. 'Right.' Lockie opened the door and slid from the station wagon. 'I'll see you back at the house later.'

And Georgia could only sit there as her brother walked away. Before she could move, unclip her centre seat belt and slip into Lockie's now vacant place by the door, Jarrod pulled the station wagon away from the kerb. She was left sitting close to Jarrod, as close as lovers. The way they used to...

Once again her brother had neatly sidestepped any responsibilities.

'I'm sorry about all this—' Georgia strove to keep her voice even '—and I appreciate your helping us out,' she finished quickly.

'As I said, it's no sweat.' He was frowning, and they lapsed into an uncomfortable silence until Georgia had to direct him to turn off the highway.

The flats were old but well kept and they had no trouble finding the right one, for Morgan was standing in the lighted open doorway watching for them. As Georgia climbed out of the car she came hurrying down the path, suitcase in hand.

'Georgia! Thank goodness you're here. I thought Steve would come back before you finished. I've got my things. Let's go,' she finished breathlessly.

'Just a minute, Morgan.' Georgia stopped her sister's head-long flight with a hand on her arm. 'I think we should go inside and wait for Steve and you can explain exactly what happened.'

'When we get home, Georgia. I'll tell you then. I don't want to see Steve or stay here any longer, and what's more I'm not going to.'

'Only a couple of weeks ago you couldn't bear to be any-where else,' Georgia reminded her sister wearily.

Morgan turned on her, her darkish curls flouncing. 'And I might have known you'd throw that up at me, Georgia. You think I'm still a child, but I'm not a child!' She stamped her foot.

'Morgan—' Georgia went to put her hand on her sister's shoulder but the younger girl brushed it away.

'I'm not staying, Georgia. You don't even care that I'll probably have a black eye tomorrow. Oh, come on. I'll get the rest of my stuff later. Let's go.' She reached for the car-door catch.

Jarrod had walked around the car by now and he took the case from Morgan before opening the door for her.

'For heaven's sake.' The young girl noticed him for the first time. 'I don't believe it. Jarrod Maclean.'

He inclined his head. 'One and the same. I'm sorry we're not meeting in better circumstances.'

'Well, yes.' Morgan shot a swift glance at Georgia before

smiling a little unsteadily. 'You don't look a day older and it must be—what, four years?'

'More or less. And perhaps you should save that, "You don't look a day older," until you see me in broad daylight rather than under a dull streetlight.'

Morgan laughed then, relaxing. 'You're still more of a hunk than you have a right to be. And I guess I look a bit different from when you last saw me too.'

'Yes, you're all grown-up—without your school uniform and your ankle socks.'

'I'm about the same age Georgia was when you came home from college, aren't I?'

The air about them thickened and Georgia's knuckles whitened as she clenched her fists.

'Round about.' Jarrod's reply was flatly casual.

'That's the trouble with families.' Morgan wrinkled her nose at Jarrod. 'They've all seen you at your worst and they aren't above reminding you about it either.'

'Morgan.' Georgia's voice sounded thin to her ears.

'Especially big sisters,' Morgan remarked as she slid into the front seat of the car.

Jarrod was still holding the door open and Georgia could only climb into the car herself. After closing the door, Jarrod deposited Morgan's case in the back of the wagon and climbed into the driver's seat.

'How long have you been home?' Morgan asked him as he set the car in motion.

'Almost a week.'

'Georgia told me Uncle Peter had had another heart attack so I guess that's why you've come home.'

'That's right.'

'The last I heard, you were in the States. What I wouldn't give to go somewhere exciting like that. And what a bore to have to come back here.'

'Morgan...' Georgia tried to stem the flow of her sister's bubbling conversation.

'Well, it is boring. What's to do around here?'

Georgia sighed.

'But, Jarrod—' Morgan put her hand on his arm '—I'm sorry about Uncle Peter. I always liked him,' she said sincerely.

Georgia barely heard her. She sat suddenly tense, a play of bewildering emotions momentarily pushing her worries about Morgan's lack of tact out of her mind. Morgan's small hand seemed to glow where it rested on Jarrod's arm, its paleness in stark contrast to his tanned skin. What could be happening to her? She wanted to reach out and pull Morgan's hand away.

'I know Georgia visits Uncle Peter every week,' Morgan was saying, 'but I bet he's pleased to see *you* back home.'

Georgia forcibly tore her gaze from Morgan's hand and shifted guiltily on the seat. It had been well over a week since she'd seen Uncle Peter. Not since he'd dropped his bombshell about Jarrod's return and she'd run like a startled rabbit.

She should have known with his father being so ill that Jarrod would come home, but for some reason—self-delusional—it hadn't occurred to her. And it hadn't been only Uncle Peter's obvious pleasure at his son's imminent return that had had her heart aching. She'd been caught unawares and she'd taken flight, not returning to the Maclean house in case she ran into Jarrod and made a complete fool of herself.

Sitting here beside him only emphasised how easy that would be for her to do.

'How is he now?' Morgan asked, and Jarrod shrugged slightly.

'He's a little better, according to the doctor, but the last attack he had took its toll on him. That's why Isabel sent for me.'

There was an edge to his voice when he mentioned his stepmother and Georgia also tensed, blanketing the memories before they could take hold of her.

When Georgia had been a child the Macleans, Peter and Isabel, had always confused her with their relationship. They were cool, restrained, never laughed together the way her parents did. And when Jarrod joined the family she had felt sorry for the tall, lanky teenager who had come to live in that quiet, unemotional atmosphere.

Isabel Maclean was Georgia's mother's older sister, yet the two sisters couldn't have been more dissimilar. Georgia's mother had been bright and effervescent, loving and caring. Isabel rarely so much as smiled, and Georgia couldn't remember her aunt ever hugging any of them when they were children.

After Jarrod had arrived Georgia had always sensed that although Isabel and her stepson never openly expressed their dislike it was a mutual emotion. Or so she'd thought.

She recalled asking him once what he thought of Isabel and he had retreated into himself, shutting her out. Until she'd slid hot kisses along the line of his square jaw to nibble teasingly on his earlobe. Then he'd turned to her, his arms holding her almost desperately to him, kissing her with a fierce passion that had at first frightened and then inflamed her.

'And how's Aunt Isabel coping with Uncle Peter's last attack?' Morgan asked.

'With her usual self-possession,' Jarrod replied evenly.

'She's a cold fish, that's for sure.'

'Morgan!' Georgia reprimanded her sister.

'Well, she is, Georgia. She's always been like that. When I was a kid I used to wonder what she'd do if I climbed on her knee and put my sticky fingers on her dress, but I was never game to find out.' Morgan giggled. 'I reckon she'd have passed out if I had. She wasn't a bit like our mother. You'd never have known they were sisters, would you, Jarrod?'

'No, I suppose not.' Jarrod turned off the highway and Georgia sensed an even deeper undercurrent in his flat tone.

'But then again,' Morgan continued, 'you'd never guess Georgia and I were sisters. Georgia is the image of Mum and Lockie's fair like Dad.' She gave a soft laugh. 'I'm somewhere in the middle. And, speaking of Lockie, where is our dear brother anyway?'

'Collecting his van from Andy's,' Georgia told her. 'Or, at least, he was,' she added as Jarrod drew to a halt in the driveway behind Lockie's van. 'He's actually beaten us home.'

The outside light flicked on, illuminating the path, and as they climbed the steps Lockie opened the door.

'Great timing!' he exclaimed. 'You OK, Morgan?'

'I'm fine now, Lockie,' Morgan assured him with a faintly martyred air.

Jarrod set down her suitcase and Lockie turned to him. 'Hey, thanks for stepping in and helping us out, mate.'

'Yes, poor Jarrod.' Morgan pulled a face. 'Only back a week and you're already rescuing the Grayson family again. Dad told me when Lockie was young you were always saving him from all sorts of scrapes. Georgia too.'

Jarrod laughed easily and Georgia's nerve-endings vibrated elatedly. 'As a boy Lockie had the very worst luck of anyone I knew for being caught out by his father or mine.'

'And when Georgia was late she just used to say she was with you and Dad accepted it without question.' Lockie laughed with him.

Oh, Lockie. Georgia swallowed painfully. She'd always said she was with Jarrod because it had been the truth.

'Georgia staying out late at night?' Morgan put her hands on her hips. 'I'd forgotten about that. Ha! You can hardly dictate to me, then, can you? Or is it the old, Do as I say not as I do?' She smirked at her sister. 'You're blushing, Georgia. That's what comes of having a shady past.'

Georgia's vocal cords refused point-blank to function and for the life of her she couldn't conjure up a light retort. She shot a quick, desperate glance at her brother and saw that his face had coloured too. She didn't dare look at Jarrod.

Lockie broke into the lengthening silence. 'Well, you know what they say, Morgan—it's the quiet ones you have to watch. And no one could call you quiet. But anyway,' he continued quickly before she could interject, 'what's all this rubbish about Steve hitting you?'

'He did hit me. Look.' She indicated a slightly reddened mark on her cheekbone. 'But don't worry—I hit him right back. Then he just walked out. End of story.'

Lockie raised his eyebrows. 'What was the fight about?'

'Nothing. And everything.' Morgan pursed her lips. 'He's pig-headed and obstinate.'

'You should know about that, Morgan. Pig-headed and obstinate? Then that makes two of you,' Lockie remarked drily.

'Don't you start, Lockie.' Morgan pouted. 'I've already had enough from Georgia. And I really don't care to face the big-brother, big-sister inquisition tonight. I didn't get any sleep last night and I'm tired. We'll talk in the morning, maybe. I think I'll go to bed now.' She turned back to Jarrod and the sulky look left her pretty face. 'No one around here understands me,' she murmured with a sigh. 'I can sympathise with you, Jarrod. I'd cut and run if I had the chance too.' And with a flounce she left them.

Lockie grimaced at Jarrod and picked up his sister's suitcase. 'Give us strength! How about some coffee? I could do with a shot of caffeine and I put the kettle on just before you arrived home. Want a cup, Jarrod?'

He inclined his head. 'Thanks.'

Georgia moved towards the kitchen and to her consternation Jarrod followed her, watching silently as she set out the coffee-mugs.

Flashes of conversation came disjointedly back.

'Isabel sent for me.'

'You're still more of a hunk than you have a right to be.'

'I'm about the same age Georgia was...'

And with torturous clarity she saw again Morgan's small hand on Jarrod's arm.

'How's the coffee coming?' Lockie appeared behind Jarrod, fragmenting the atmosphere of solid tension in the kitchen. 'Morgan's decided she's not going to bed and she'll have a cup too,' he added, rolling his eyes towards the ceiling, and Georgia automatically reached for another mug.

When she'd poured hot water over the coffee grains she set the steaming mugs on a tray, but before she could lift it Jarrod had taken the tray and motioned for her to precede him into the living room.

Morgan was already in the room and had draped herself over a chair. As Jarrod passed her a mug of coffee she smiled up at him.

'Thanks, Jarrod.' Her young voice was softly husky. 'I suppose you've noticed a few changes around the area,' she continued brightly. 'The new shopping complex and then all the houses that seem to be sprouting up like mushrooms.'

'Well, he has been away for four years, Morgan,' Lockie said scornfully. 'And I'm more interested in the States. Tell us about that, Jarrod.'

He shrugged and sat down. 'Not much to tell really. I've been working pretty hard.'

'That's sacrilegious!' Morgan exclaimed, and her glance slid to her sister. 'You sound like Georgia. That's all she ever does. Work, work and more work.'

Georgia sank wearily onto the sofa, yearning for the solitude of her bed, the oblivion of sleep. 'You're exaggerating, Morgan.'

'And it's a pity you don't do a bit of work.' Lockie frowned at his younger sister. 'Instead of swanning around with your friends all day.'

A flush washed Morgan's cheeks and she sent Lockie a withering look. 'I don't swan around. And jobs aren't exactly thick on the ground around here, brother dear.'

'We know that, Morgan,' Georgia put in placatingly, but before she could continue Morgan held up her hand.

'I can feel a lecture coming on so I think I will go to bed after all.' She stood up and set her coffee-mug on the table with a bang. 'You know, I really think you two will be disappointed if I don't go and get myself into mega-trouble.' She flounced out of the room.

Lockie muttered under his breath. 'Seems to me Steve and Morgan are quite prepared to play at being grown-ups but they're too young emotionally to handle the situation they've got themselves into.' He paused and turned, frowning, to Georgia. 'Into trouble? You don't think she's taking drugs or—well, that she could be...?'

Georgia's hands tightened on her coffee-mug, her knuckles whitening with tension. Her gaze rose to meet Lockie's and he reddened, his eyes falling from hers.

'No. Of course, she wouldn't be that stupid,' he contradicted himself quickly, and gave a nervous laugh. 'Anyway, enough of Morgan. I'm sure you don't want to hear all this, Jarrod.' He glanced back at his sister. 'Never a dull moment around here, is there, Georgia? And you must be exhausted, arriving home from a hard day at work then having to go racing out to bring Morgan home.'

Georgia nodded and took a gulp of her coffee. It wasn't work or the drama with their sister that was responsible for her feeling like a piece of chewed string.

If only she was on her own so she could rationally evaluate her reactions. Yet how could she have known just how radically the reappearance of Jarrod Maclean would affect her? Because, as much as she wished she could deny it, the fact was that he did still have the power to turn her emotions upside down.

She could see herself at seventeen again. That had been when Jarrod had come home after graduating. Georgia had been playing tennis and had been hot and dishevelled from the long cycle home. She'd walked in and he'd been there, in that same chair. When she'd entered the room he'd stood up, and he was a good four inches taller than her brother. Her eyes had lifted too, over his long, lithe body, to meet those fantastic blue eyes.

From beneath her lowered lashes Georgia watched Jarrod

take a sip of his coffee, his strong neck muscles working as he swallowed.

Did he remember too? Probably not. Why would he?

'What were we talking about?' Lockie continued. 'Oh, yes. The changes around here.'

'I thought I'd taken the wrong exit when I headed out along the highway the day I arrived,' Jarrod remarked easily. 'But once I turned onto that road outside I knew I was back. At least our little bit has stayed the same.'

Lockie's eyes ran over the high-ceilinged lounge of their large old house. 'Mmm. Lucky your father never had to sell off his land. Minus this little plot he sold to our father. Fifty acres, isn't it?'

Jarrod nodded.

Georgia's nervous system felt as if it had been constricted into a tight block, shaky and volatile. How could the three of them be sitting here so amicably discussing something as mundane as this while the awful events of four years ago sat with them?

'They must have been good friends back then, Dad and Uncle Peter,' Lockie was saying. 'I mean for Uncle Peter to sell our father and mother this place.'

At that particular moment Georgia's eyes were on Jarrod's hands and with a shock she watched his knuckles whiten as his fingers tightened around his coffee-mug. Her gaze flew to his face and she saw a flicker of a nerve beating in his suddenly tensed jaw.

What could have sparked off his reaction? Surely he didn't begrudge her parents this land? After all, Geoff Grayson had bought this house and had had it moved onto this block at least ten years before anyone had been aware that Jarrod even existed.

Georgia continued to surreptitiously watch him but his long lashes now safely shielded the expression in his eyes. He seemed intent on the remains of the coffee in his mug.

'Of course this place needs a few running repairs now,'

Lockie continued easily. 'Dad's always just about to start on it when he gets a job working on someone else's place. I've promised to give him a hand to paint the outside when he gets back from the coast. And the wiring needs attention too.'

Jarrod smiled stiffly, crossing one long denim-clad leg over the other, the rasp of the thick material echoing loudly to Georgia's sensitised hearing, and she swallowed.

'These old colonial styles are beautiful but there's quite a bit of upkeep on them,' he said evenly.

'And how.' Lockie glanced at his wrist-watch and when the phone rang he grinned broadly. 'Right on time. That'll be Mandy. She said she'd ring to let me know she'd arrived safely. If you'll excuse me, Jarrod, I'll take it on the extension in the kitchen.' He stood up and raced along the hallway.

Georgia blinked in surprise at Lockie's sudden exit. Her brother really was the limit. Leaving her alone with Jarrod was developing into a harrowing habit. She shifted uncomfortably on her seat.

'Mandy, Lockie's fiancée, flew home to New Zealand today to visit her family,' she got out. 'I suppose you met her last time you called in.'

He shook his head. 'No, she was working. But Lockie told me they were engaged.'

'She's very nice. Everyone likes her. She's become part of the family.' Georgia knew she was babbling inanely but couldn't seem to stop herself. 'They plan to marry later in the year.'

'I'm surprised. At Lockie tying himself down,' he expanded. 'Even though he's—what, nearly twenty-eight? Somehow I find it hard to cast Lockie in the role of family man.'

Georgia caught back the bitter laugh that rose inside her. She'd been prepared to settle down with him when he had been younger than Lockie was now.

'But I guess I'm four years behind. I'm afraid I still see Lockie as a gangling youth with a guitar.' He smiled faintly and Georgia couldn't prevent her eyes from shifting to meet his. And she was held captive by the achingly familiar wonder of his attraction.

She was mesmerised by the shape of his mouth, the upward tilt of the corners, the white slash of strong teeth against his tanned skin, the two creases that deepened when he smiled, running furrows in his cheeks. And she wanted to follow their course with the tip of her tongue, follow them right to the corners of his mouth and within. Georgia dragged her libidinous thoughts back from that so dangerous ground.

'It's incredible how quickly the years pass.'

'Is it?' The bitter words were out before she had consciously formed them and he looked across at her, suddenly still. Georgia forced herself to relax a little. 'I thought it was only elderly people who complained about that,' she added quickly with a forced-sounding laugh.

His mouth twisted in self-mockery. 'Then perhaps I'm getting old.'

That same awkward silence fell between them and Georgia took a sip of her now lukewarm coffee.

'Peter missed you this week,' he said softly, his words taking her by surprise.

'I'm sorry.' Her eyes flitted about the room. 'I've been fairly busy, and with you coming home—well, I...' She shrugged.

'You didn't want to take a chance on running into me,' he finished quietly.

'Don't be silly.' Georgia flushed guiltily. 'Why would I feel like that? I thought your father would want time alone with you. And, as I said, I've just been busy.'

'Yes, it seems you have. I've been here twice and missed you both times.' He slid his empty coffee-mug onto the tray and stood up, taking a couple of stiff-legged strides across the carpet. 'We had to meet eventually, Georgia. Surely you knew that?' he said flatly.

'Of course I knew.' She swallowed, her mouth dry. 'Really, Jarrod, you're reading far more into this than is there.'

'Am I, Georgia?' He turned back to her, folding his strong arms across his chest. The worn denim of his jeans pulled tautly across his thighs, and she felt her heartbeats quicken in that old familiar way.

And it was familiar, she realised with total shock. Although in four years no man had touched on those intoxicating emotions, suddenly the years slid away as though they'd never been and she was physically alert to the muscular nuances of his body, the deep tone of his voice. Georgia's mouth dried as panic rose inside her. Not again, she admonished herself. She wasn't going to let him hurt her again.

'I'm sorry, Georgia.' He sighed. 'You know if it hadn't been for Peter I wouldn't have come back. I had no control over that.'

Georgia's heart twisted painfully. Well, she told herself brutally, if she was harbouring any illusions about his return she'd be advised to nip them in the bud before they grew to envelop her again. There had never been any chance that he had returned to her. How could she be so foolish to imagine he might have? Even if she'd wanted him to...

'But as I am here—well,' he continued with a grimace, 'like it or not, we're going to run into each other once in a while.'

'That needn't be often,' she said with an evenness she was proud of. 'I suppose you've taken over your father's business, so you'll probably be working, and so will I. I can visit your father when you're at the office so we needn't see each other at all.' She steeled herself to hold his gaze.

A pulse flickered in his jaw. 'If that's what you want.'

Georgia swallowed. What she wanted was to wipe away the four years and that fateful night, have everything back to normal between them. His love. Her belief in his integrity. So many things. But that was impossible.

She pushed herself to her feet and stood facing him, her chin held high. 'I think perhaps that might be best, Jarrod, considering—well...' She shrugged uneasily.

'Considering?' His blue eyes had narrowed.

'Considering all that...' Georgia paused again '...all that happened. I'm a lot older now, and a lot wiser. So please don't worry that I might make another distasteful scene. That's all behind me.'

His eyes burned into hers across the few feet separating them. 'I don't recall saying that you would, Georgia.' He ran a strong hand through his dark hair. 'Look, we used to be friends. Let's start again and try to at least be civil to each other.'

His deep voice struck more raw and tender chords and Georgia bit off a sharp, incredulous laugh. 'Civil? I'm sure we can. You. Me. And Aunt Isabel.'

CHAPTER THREE

JARROD'S lips thinned and a faint flush seemed to colour the line of his high cheekbones.

'I don't intend to defend myself again, Georgia. I've done more than enough of that. Perhaps I was asking too much for us to leave the past where it is, behind us. But I would have liked you and me to remain friends,' he said slowly, as though he was having trouble forming the words, and then he sighed. 'It's late. I guess I should be going. I've got an early start in the morning. Peter wants me to visit the Gold Coast branch.'

You used to take me with you. Georgia longed to say the words. Her eyes rested on him, her breathing becoming shallow as more old memories rose to haunt her. No! Concentrate on now, she instructed herself angrily. But the present meant looking at him, drinking in the tall length of him.

His body came the closest to perfection of any man's she'd ever seen. Those strong legs, muscular thighs, narrow hips, taut buttocks, straight back, broad, well-built shoulders, solid arms that wrapped around you, making you feel safe and warm and wanted.

Georgia swallowed painfully, her fingers curling into her palms. Forget the past, she told herself with feeling. And forget his body. That was all he was. A body. Part of a yesterday she didn't need to remember.

He had moved towards the door, but when he stepped into the hallway he stopped, turning back to face her. 'Say goodbye to Lockie for me. And Georgia, at least come and see Peter. He misses you.'

With that he was gone.

Later Georgia fell into bed, expecting to lie awake, but exhaustion won out and she slept deeply, without having to think about Jarrod Maclean and the disturbing knowledge that the effect he had on her was just as devastating as it used to be.

'Georgia! Hey, Georgia!' Lockie called as he bounded up the front steps.

'Why does he have to be so noisy?' Morgan muttered to no one in particular. She was lounging in a chair, idly flipping through a glossy magazine.

It was just a week since the night Jarrod had driven Georgia to collect Morgan and things were gradually settling back into a relative degree of normality. Not that they had made much headway with Morgan. She was unusually subdued and flatly refused to discuss anything with anyone, even Steve, who tried to phone her each day. All she would say was that Steve had suggested they get engaged and she hadn't wanted to be committed to him or anyone.

Jarrod they hadn't seen, and Georgia told herself she was very thankful for that fact. She could almost convince herself that she'd imagined his return, that there was still the width of the Pacific Ocean safely between them.

'Georgia?' Lockie repeated.

'What's wrong now?' Georgia glanced up at her brother as he burst into the living room. She was trying to finish an assignment for part of her course in business management.

'Bloody everything!' Lockie threw himself into a chair.

'Swearing won't help.' Georgia smiled faintly at him.

'Maybe not. But it relieves my tension. Want to hear the good news or the bad news?' He sighed loudly and sat forward, resting his elbows on his knees, his chin on his hand. 'I should be over the moon about this but...'

Georgia raised her eyebrows, glancing across at Morgan before turning back to Lockie. 'But? And over the moon about what?'

'About the booking I just got for Country Blues,' Lockie told them.

'What booking is that?' Georgia's mind was still on her assignment, so she was only giving Lockie part of her attention.

'*The* booking, Georgia. The one I've been after. The one you told me to go out and get.'

Georgia looked up at him then. 'The one I told—? You mean the Country Music Club in Ipswich?'

Lockie nodded and beamed from ear to ear.

'Hey! That's great, Lockie.' Morgan made a thumbs-up sign.

'Yes, Lockie, that's wonderful,' Georgia agreed.

'You're telling me! I walked in and they took us on. Well—' Lockie looked a little sheepish '—it wasn't quite that easy. I've been working on them all week. It turns out the band they had booked had a car accident or something and had to cry off at the last minute. Bad luck for them but fantastic for us. I was in the right place at the right time for once.'

'It must have been fate,' Morgan retorted drily, but Lockie ignored her.

'It's our big chance, Georgia. We've worked damn hard to get it and we were due for a lucky break. It's what all the practising and the taking of those bit engagements has been all about.' He rubbed his hands together. 'There's no telling where this booking could lead. The Country Music Club is the first place anyone who's anyone will look.'

'So what's the bad news you mentioned?' Georgia queried. 'What could possibly be bad about that?'

'The bad news is we have to start Friday night and Mandy's still in New Zealand.' He stood up and paced the floor. 'Where the hell am I going to get a replacement singer at this late date? Good ones sure don't grow on trees.'

'Can't you manage without Mandy?' Georgia asked sympathetically.

'Probably. But you know how it is. We're just starting to

make our name. With a female lead. Besides, the band needs a good-looking bird to give everyone something to look at apart from our ugly faces.' He stood up, legs apart, his hands on his hips. 'I mean, our music's great, I really believe in it, but the whole programme we've been working on for over a year depends on a girl up front. The boys are going to love this when I tell them. Blast Mandy!'

Morgan closed her magazine and threw it on the coffee-table. 'If you like I'll volunteer to don a skimpy outfit and stand up there on stage for you, but I somehow can't see me thrilling everyone if I open my mouth and try to sing.'

Lockie gave a reluctant laugh. Morgan's tone-deafness was a family joke and Georgia joined in their laughter.

'If you rang Mandy couldn't she fly back in time?'

'I tried. She's not there.'

'Then surely you could find someone to stand in for Mandy till she gets back?' she said, smiling up at her brother, and his eyes narrowed on her.

'Just a minute,' he breathed. 'I've got it. We're saved.' He raised his eyes skyward in thankfulness. 'I don't know why I didn't think of it right away. *You* can fill in for Mandy on Friday night, Georgia.'

Georgia stared at him blankly and then shook her head. 'Oh, no. Not me, Lockie. We've been through all this before Mandy joined Country Blues. You know how I feel about performing in public. And, in case you hadn't noticed, I already have a job, at the bookshop.'

Her brother held up his hand.

'No, Lockie,' Georgia repeated adamantly. 'I like singing— I won't deny that. I used to enjoy it. But privately, not on any stage.'

'Georgia, please.' Lockie came over to stand in front of her. 'It would only be for two nights. Then we'd have all of next week to get in touch with Mandy and talk her into coming back early.'

'Try phoning Mandy again. She could easily be back here

by Friday,' Georgia told him, and Lockie threw his hands in the air.

'I told you she wasn't there. Don't you think I phoned her as soon as I got the job? I did. Her mother says she's gone off touring and then she'll end up in the back woods somewhere visiting cousins. They can't contact her until Sunday anyway, so there's no way she'll make it back.'

'I'm sorry, Lockie.'

'Georgia, you know all the songs. You know the band. You've jammed with us often enough. And I reckon Mandy's costume would even fit you; you're about the same size.'

'Well, almost,' Morgan put in amusedly, and Lockie shot a warning glance at her.

'But I don't care for singing in front of an audience,' Georgia reiterated firmly, standing up so that her brother didn't have the advantage of his height looming over her.

'Look, Georgia—' Lockie's hands clasped her shoulders '—you're great, if only you'd realise it. Haven't we always said that? Almost as good as Mandy. Isn't that the truth, Morgan?'

'Better than Mandy,' Morgan remarked, and Lockie decided to let that go and turned back to his other sister.

'I know you can do it. You *are* great.'

Georgia shrugged her brother's hands off. 'Don't try to sweet-talk me, Lockie. And don't pressure me.'

'Sweet-talk you!' Lockie muttered something under his breath. 'OK, let me put it like this, Georgia. Friday night is our big chance. And you know what Mandy said. No more two-bit jobs. Well, I've pulled off the best—an engagement at the Country Music Club.

'But now I've got it we need a female lead. It won't be Country Blues without one. Surely you can see that? You're the only one besides Mandy who knows our arrangements. We'd only need to run through them with you tomorrow evening and you'd be right for Friday night.'

'I can't do it, Lockie. I'm sorry.'

'Morgan, you talk to her.' Lockie appealed to his younger sister. 'Make her see sense.'

'Don't bring me into it, Lockie. She's the one who has to get up in front of all those people and sing.'

'You're a great help.' Lockie ran his hand through his hair.

Georgia sighed exasperatedly. 'I haven't got the time, Lockie. And I have late shifts at the bookshop. It would never work.'

'It's only Friday and Saturday, Georgia. I know you only work late on Thursday nights.'

'Substituting singers doesn't sound legal to me—' Georgia began.

'I'll tell them at the club, keep it all above board,' Lockie put in quickly. 'And Mandy can be back for next weekend's gig. So where's the problem? Two nights only, Georgia.'

'Lockie, please!' Georgia brushed her fingers across her forehead.

'Yes, Lockie, I think you've badgered Georgia enough for one night,' Morgan intervened with an uncharacteristic concern. 'Why don't you sleep on it, Georgia? And tomorrow, if you feel the same, then that will be it. Lockie will just have to find someone else. OK?'

Georgia acquiesced and with a heartfelt sigh Lockie did the same.

'All right,' he agreed. 'I need a cup of coffee and then I guess I should be off too. I'll have to put the other guys in the picture.' With a last appealing glance at his sister he went into the kitchen.

'What will you do?' Morgan asked.

'I've always held out on this with Lockie,' Georgia said dispiritedly. 'Ever since we were teenagers and he formed his first band he's wanted me to sing with him. I enjoyed it for a while, but—' She stopped. But then Jarrod had arrived back and singing with her brother's band had faded into a very poor second behind being with Jarrod, being held in his arms, making love…

'If getting up on stage makes you so nervous—well—' Morgan shrugged '—there's no point in making more hassles for yourself. Still, I can see Lockie's point. It's a pity Mandy had to be in New Zealand now, just when Lockie's got the band such a big break.'

Georgia nodded and slowly followed Lockie into the kitchen to begin preparing the evening meal. Lockie sat dejectedly at the table, staring into his mug of coffee.

He glanced up at his sister. 'Georgia, we need the money the Country Music Club will bring,' he said in a low voice.

'Now come on, Lockie, I know we aren't rich but we're hardly destitute.'

Lockie's face creased in a worried frown. '*I* need the money, Georgia.' He paused as she looked at him, surprised by his serious tone. 'You know the van's under hire purchase? Well, I'm behind with the payments. It will be repossessed if I don't catch up with it.'

'Oh, Lockie.' Georgia shook her head. 'Why didn't you tell me? I could help—'

Lockie held up his hand. 'No, Georgia. It's my responsibility.' He sighed. 'And there's Mandy. Do you think I like putting off our wedding? She deserves better than that. I want to be able to make it up to her for the last penny-scrimping year.'

Georgia could feel the tension in him.

'This is a big-time gig, Georgia, and it pays big time. We won't have to be counting every cent if we can pull this off,' he persisted. 'Not Mandy and me. Not Andy and the boys. And not you. We'll pay you for Friday and Saturday nights, and as you're saving for a new car this will boost your bank account, believe me.'

'Lockie—'

'And Dad. Maybe we can send him on a holiday. He hasn't had one since Mum died. Then there's Morgan. We could help her out with a secretarial course. It would make such a difference; don't you see?'

'I see you using emotional blackmail,' Georgia said tiredly.

'Two performances, Georgia. That's all I ask. I'll talk to Mandy and she'll come back. Please, Georgia?'

'Oh, Lockie.' She sighed. 'All right,' she agreed weakly. 'But two performances only.'

Lockie's thin face broke into a grin. 'Thanks, Georgia. You don't know how much this means to me.' He stood up and gave her a bear hug. 'I'm off to sort out a plan of attack with the boys. Just stick my dinner in the oven. See you later.'

And later, with the dishes done, she returned to the living room and her assignment. It was particularly extensive and she decided to take advantage of the peace and quiet of the empty house. Morgan had gone out with friends and Lockie hadn't returned since their discussion about Georgia's performing with the band.

Soon she was involved in her research and she actually jumped in fright when a decisive knock sounded on the door. She glanced tentatively through the lattice panel to check on the caller before she opened the door, and her heart flipped in her chest. Jarrod. What could he want? Slowly she unlocked the door and swung it open.

'Hello, Georgia,' he greeted her softly, the veranda light highlighting the slight wave in his dark hair.

'I'm afraid Lockie isn't here,' she began, and sensed him stiffen.

'That doesn't matter. Can I come in?' he asked levelly.

Georgia paused and then stepped back, leaving the door open and preceding him into the living room. Without looking at him she collected her books and papers together and stacked them on the coffee-table.

He picked up a book, glanced at the title and raised his eyebrows. 'Heavy reading.'

'Research for my course,' she told him without elaboration, and sank onto the edge of her chair.

'You're studying business administration?'

Georgia nodded. 'I hope to finish next year. Did you want

to see Lockie about anything in particular? I'm afraid I don't know when he'll be home.' And it would be just like Lockie to pick this evening to be late, she reflected silently.

'I'd prefer to talk to you about it.' He replaced the book on the pile and sat down opposite her.

Could he hear her heartbeats thundering in her chest? she wondered, and fought to keep her expression bland. What could they possibly have to discuss?

'It's about Morgan,' he continued. 'Does she have a job yet?'

Georgia shook her head.

'We may have a vacancy coming up in the office at Ipswich in a few weeks' time and I thought she might be interested. Does she have any secretarial or computer training?'

'Only what she's done at school.'

'If she's prepared to go to night courses the job's hers.'

'Thank you,' Georgia said slowly. 'But you didn't have to—'

'I know I didn't have to, Georgia,' he cut in a little irritatedly, 'but it's a genuine offer. It's up to Morgan if she wants it or not. If she is interested she can come and see me about it.'

'All right. I'll tell her.'

'I also made some enquiries about her boyfriend, young Steve Gordon.'

'Oh.' Georgia looked across at him.

'He seems a level-headed young bloke. His foreman says he's one of the best apprentices we've got.'

'I like him.' Georgia tried to relax, leaning back in her seat, sliding her hands into the pockets of her trousers when she realised she was unconsciously clasping and unclasping her fingers. But she sat up, tense again, when she felt Jarrod's gaze fall on the rise of her breasts as they thrust against the thin material of her cotton shirt. She pushed herself to her feet and began straightening her papers to cover her discomposure.

'Did Morgan explain what happened that night at the flat?' he asked, after the strained moment had passed.

'No. And no one can get any sensible explanation out of her. I've tried, and so has Lockie.' Georgia sighed. 'She's something of a handful, I'm afraid.'

'Has Lockie talked to Steve?'

Georgia glanced up at him and then away again. Why did he feel he had to concern himself with their affairs? Didn't he think they could get by without his wise counsel?

'Of course,' she replied sharply. 'Steve maintains he didn't intentionally hit Morgan. They'd had an argument and he swung around in anger, threw his arms up and accidentally caught her on the side of the face. He assured me he felt terrible about it but Morgan wouldn't and still won't accept his apologies.'

Georgia sighed again and turned quietly away from him— away from the unconscious magnetic appeal of him that reached out to her, began to entangle her in its seductive tentacles. 'They'll just have to work it out themselves if they want to be together,' she finished flatly.

'Do you want me to talk to Steve?'

'No.' Georgia lifted her chin and faced him again. 'There's no need for you to get involved. We can sort it out and, really, Morgan's the one who has to decide what she's going to do about it.'

'I suppose so.' Jarrod frowned. 'She just seems so young.'

As young as she herself had been when she'd fallen in love with him, Georgia thought bitterly, and two years later he had been the one to do the hurting. He had shown no signs then of concern for her, for the havoc he had created in her life, so what right had he to be so solicitous about Morgan?

The silence stretched for immeasurable seconds—seconds that were a torture for Georgia. She despised him... Yet at the same time she yearned to turn back to him, have him hold her the way he used to do.

And she felt momentarily forlorn, dispirited, wanting to

share her burdens with him, her worries about Morgan's rebelliousness, about Lockie's financial problems which meant he had to postpone his marriage to Mandy, about her guilty reluctance to sing with Country Blues. But mostly she wanted to share with him her own loss—the loss that was still part of her...and her pain.

No! She very nearly screamed at herself. She couldn't trust him. Not ever. He'd only betray her trust and let her down again.

Jarrod's sigh brought her back to awareness and she realised he'd left the chair, moved away from her to stand gazing out through the open window into the darkness. 'I'd forgotten how quiet it was out here. After living in a big city the stillness is almost deafening.'

Georgia found herself studying his profile. It was exactly as she remembered it. Where he was concerned she appeared to possess a photographic memory. After all he'd done.

'It's amazing the things—normal everyday things—you remember when you're away from home.' He gave a wry laugh. 'Do you know what I remembered most?'

Unable to speak, Georgia shook her head, while inside she cried out, No, she didn't know what he remembered most, but she knew what he forgot.

'The sound of the storm-bird. Every time the sky grew overcast and it turned cool, I'd be reminded of the storm-bird. When I was a kid I used to think its cry was the saddest sound I ever heard.'

So the forlorn bird's cry, supposedly heralding the coming storm, was his fondest memory? Georgia's lips twisted embitteredly. But then why should he remember a passionate, obviously physical affair with a gauche, gullible young woman who'd idolised him?

'Thanks for going to see Peter last night,' he said, when Georgia made no attempt to continue the conversation.

She shrugged and sat down again. 'He was surprisingly well. Aunt Isabel said he'd had a comfortable day. I don't suppose there's any chance he'll…' Georgia left the question hanging and Jarrod shook his head.

'The doctor says it's only a matter of time. He's had twenty-five years they said he wouldn't have after his bad accident over in Western Australia so he considers he's been lucky.'

'I'm sorry, Jarrod,' Georgia said, wishing the words didn't sound so banal.

'These things happen.'

They both looked up as the sound of a car broke into their mutual preoccupation. And the silence continued as footsteps rattled up the stairs.

'Jarrod! Hi! Been here long?' Lockie asked brightly. He shot a quick, assessing glance from Jarrod standing with his back to the window to Georgia sitting stiffly on the edge of her chair.

'Not long.' Jarrod shoved his hands in his pockets. 'I guess you've been practising. How's the band going?'

'Just great.' Lockie's eyes lit up. 'Did Georgia tell you I've pulled off a fantastic booking? At the Country Music Club. It used to be Rusty's. Remember it?'

Jarrod nodded.

'It could be a major stepping-stone to—well, to anything. The sky's the limit.' Lockie rubbed his hands together. 'If we make a good impression at the Country Music Club we could hit the big time. What do you say, Georgia?'

'Nashville here we come,' Georgia remarked drily, and Lockie pulled a face at her.

'Very funny, Georgia. You aren't giving this the right amount of reverence. But don't worry—I won't bear a grudge.'

'And, let me guess, you'll never forget the little people?' Jarrod smiled at him, reviving old memories. 'When's the big event?'

'Friday night.' Lockie beamed at him and sat on the arm of a chair. 'How about coming along and lending a bit of moral support?'

'Sure.'

'Great! It will be good to know at least one person will be clapping, won't it, Georgia?'

'One?' Jarrod's smile still lingered on his mouth and Georgia swallowed. 'Three, counting Georgia and Morgan, don't you mean? I suppose the whole family will be there.'

'Well, I'm not—' Georgia stopped, suddenly realising he would be in the audience when she sang with Country Blues. What would he think when he saw her up on the stage?

Jarrod had sobered, his eyes levelly on her. 'It would be a pity if you missed Lockie's big moment,' he said evenly.

'"Missed"...' Georgia repeated, and then pulled herself together. Of course. Jarrod was unaware she would be part of Country Blues. He was in for something of a shock. 'Yes, it would.'

Lockie's brows drew together and she could see that he thought she'd changed her mind about being part of the band. 'But Georgia—'

She sighed and made a negating movement with her hand. 'I'll be there, Lockie.'

He relaxed and Jarrod looked from one to the other.

Unbidden, Georgia's thoughts went back to other times Jarrod had seen her sing publicly with Lockie's band—at some local functions, the annual Jacaranda Festival, birthday parties, the local school reunion. He had frowningly told her he didn't care to share her with an audience. Of course he'd been joking. He'd laughed after he'd said it, and they'd kissed, but...

But nothing, she admonished herself. That had been years ago and she didn't need a reminder of any of it now.

'The boys are over the moon about—' Lockie began, and Georgia cut in on him.

'About the venue. So they should be. It was a real scoop on your part,' she finished quickly.

'Is it the same group you had before...?' Jarrod's almost imperceptible pause had Georgia tensing painfully. 'I went overseas?'

'No. Andy Dyne, the drummer, has been with me the long-est. He's a very colourful character, red hair and a wild beard. The other two guys have been with us for about two years,' Lockie continued. 'They're top musicians and we're all good friends, which helps. Apart from that we've all worked damn hard and we deserve this break. We could even get to do the backing on the new television show that's in the wind. That would be fantastic.'

'Television show? What are you talking about, Lockie?' Georgia raised her eyebrows.

'There's a rumour that the ABC will be making a music series, to go national and maybe even overseas. There'd be some overseas clips but it would be mostly local talent. With a regular line-dancing segment. You know how popular line-dancing is these days.' Lockie turned back to Jarrod. 'So you can imagine we're hoping.'

Thank heavens Mandy would be returning next week. The whole thing was snowballing. Television shows indeed. She frowned, worried by the conspiratorial gleam in her brother's eyes. If Lockie thought...

She ran her damp palms along the seams of her trousers, her nerves fluttering about inside her like clothes on a windy day's washing line. It was bad enough that he had invited Jarrod along on Friday night, but if her brother thought he was going to talk her into anything other than the two nights at the Country Music Club...

She swallowed again, resisting the urge to place her hand on her erratically beating heart. She simply had to forget it all until Friday night. Forget the strangers who would sit watching her. Strangers? Forget Jarrod Maclean.

If only he hadn't come back. Such a futile 'if only', she told herself. He was here now and she couldn't change that. It was her own fault for not preparing herself for his return. She would just have to keep her torturous memories at bay, weather his presence until he went back to the States.

'I got to go to the Grand Ole Opry when I was in

Tennessee,' Jarrod was telling Lockie with apparent ease, 'and I thoroughly enjoyed that.'

'Wow! I can imagine. I'm green with envy. I'd love to get to Nashville.' Lockie grimaced. 'I definitely will one day.'

'You'd have enjoyed Opryland, too. I was lucky enough to go along with a friend who was familiar with the park and its layout. Due to some precision timing we saw every show that was staged.'

How nice for you, Georgia thought, bitterness rising like bile. And was this friend female? she wanted to ask. Of course, it would have to have been. Women were always attracted to Jarrod. Apart from his tall, well-built body, he had that rare masculine magnetism that drew the female sex like moths to a naked light.

Hadn't she been enticed like the rest? And he hadn't fended her off. No, she'd had the dubious honour of being allowed to feel his warmth, to actually touch the flame. That burn had seared her very soul, singed her fragile wings so that she had never attempted to fly again.

'How nice to have a local to show you around,' she said flatly, ignoring Lockie's puzzled glance.

And her brother could look questioning. Couldn't he see she had a right to be unforgiving? While Jarrod jaunted fancy-free about the world she had had to continue on alone. Without part of herself. And him.

'It was. I kept thinking of Lockie and how he'd have been in his element.'

He was smiling and Georgia's fingers clasped tightly together in her lap.

'Do you remember those old cowboy boots you bought from someone who swore they'd belonged to Johnny Cash?' Jarrod teased Lockie. He looked relaxed, showing no outward sign that any of the past was rising to disturb him, while Georgia sat frozen in her seat.

How dared he keep mentioning the past? Yesterday was analogous with unbearable pain.

Was he totally insensitive? Didn't he remember how brutally he had severed their ties? She suppressed a twinge of guilt. Actually, she had severed the ties, but he had been the one to cause their breakup. What he'd done was unforgivable.

Her anger swelled and then ebbed a little. The pity of it was that she would have staked her life on Jarrod's integrity. She'd loved him so. And he'd betrayed that love.

'They did belong to Johnny Cash,' Lockie was protesting indignantly. 'And I've still got them.'

Jarrod laughed aloud.

'Pity they're a bit small for me now.' Lockie indicated his large foot. 'Hey, Georgia, you can wear them on Friday night for luck.'

'I'm not wearing those old boots, Lockie, not for you or anyone,' Georgia said firmly.

'Come on, Georgia, they'd look great up on stage with the lights picking out the studs.'

'Lockie!' Georgia grimaced.

'On stage?' Jarrod looked questioningly from Georgia to Lockie.

'Yes, when—' Lockie stopped and slapped his forehead theatrically. 'That's right. You don't know. Georgia is Country Blues' lead singer.'

Jarrod had sobered and his eyes bored into Georgia's, his expression one of total reproach, stirring her disturbing memories again. 'But I thought— You sing with Lockie's band?'

Georgia inclined her head. So he disapproved! She could see that by the set of his jaw, the thinned line of his lips.

'I didn't think you liked performing in public.' His eyes had narrowed, dark lashes shielding the feelings in their blue depths.

Georgia tore her eyes from his. She was a free agent, and if she wanted to dance naked on the table-tops she would do it—she had no intention of asking his permission. He wasn't her keeper and he had no right to his silent condemnation.

'That was years ago.' Georgia held his gaze. 'And a lot has changed since then.'

'Georgia is only—' Lockie began, but she cut him off.

'I'm quite looking forward to this big break,' she said quickly, avoiding Lockie's eyes. 'Lockie even has hopes of recording an album, haven't you, Lockie?'

'Yes.' Lockie took his cue from his sister. 'And, talking about albums, Ken tells me it's a known fact that D.J. Delaney of Skyrocket Records often sits in at the Country Music Club. So, who knows? It mightn't be as far-fetched as we thought. If we could only find the right material—something original to catch his attention.'

'The best of luck with it, Lockie.' Jarrod stood up. 'I guess I should be going. I'll see you both on Friday night. I'm looking forward to seeing Country Blues in action.' His eyes went to Georgia but he said nothing, simply inclining his head before he left.

'Why didn't you let me tell him you're only standing in for Mandy?' Lockie asked as Georgia closed the door.

'Was it any of his business?' she asked him shortly.

'Well, no, but—'

'I really don't see why we have to tell Jarrod Maclean everything that's going on,' Georgia bit out, and when Lockie would have replied she walked towards the kitchen. 'I'll put your dinner on the table.'

While Lockie ate his meal Georgia returned to the living room and her assignment but, try as she might, she couldn't regain her previous absorption. Her attention kept straying, and in the same direction. Jarrod Maclean.

She glanced at the time and sighed. She had an early start in the morning and as she wasn't accomplishing anything with her studies she decided she might as well go to bed. As she stood up Lockie rejoined her.

'I'm just off to bed,' she said brightly, feeling a little guilty for her earlier churlishness.

'Just a minute, Georgia.' Lockie frowned. 'I want to talk.'

She glanced at his serious expression and sat down again. 'What do you want to talk about, Lockie? If it's Friday night then I'd rather leave that until tomorrow when we run through the songs. If we discuss it tonight I might get stage fright and change my mind,' she said with a smile.

'It's not about the band.' He sat down opposite her. 'I want to talk about you. And Jarrod.'

Georgia felt her facial muscles freeze and she went to stand up. But Lockie was quicker and he motioned her back into the chair.

'Lockie, there's nothing to talk about.'

'Isn't there, Georgia?'

'No. And if there was I wouldn't want to discuss it.'

'Well, I do.' He stuck out his chin.

'Lockie, please. Not now.'

'Yes, now. While I'm all fired up and we're on our own. I think it needs to be sorted out.'

'Nothing needs to be said. Just leave it. Lockie, I'm tired—'

'No, Georgia. Look, I know you never talked about—well, any of it, back then.' He pushed himself to his feet and walked a few paces away from her before spinning back to face her. 'But, hell, Georgia! Haven't you done enough already? Can't you see what you're doing to him?'

CHAPTER FOUR

'WHAT *I'm* doing to *him*?' Georgia repeated incredulously. 'Just what am I doing to him, Lockie?'

'Well, treating him like a leper for one.'

'And how should I be treating him? Throwing myself at his feet and crying, Take me, I'm yours?'

Lockie went a little red about his ears. 'You know I didn't mean that, Georgia. I meant you haven't exactly...' He paused, searching for the right words.

'Welcomed him home with open arms?' Georgia finished. 'For heaven's sake, Lockie, do you think I'm a masochist?'

'You could be civil,' he suggested.

Civil? Hadn't Jarrod said just that? Georgia grimaced. No matter what happened, in polite society we must all be civil.

'I could be a lot of things.' Georgia couldn't keep the bitterness out of her voice.

'And you could let go of the past too.'

She gave a harsh laugh. 'I have put the past behind me. Or I had. Do you think I need Jarrod turning up to remind me of it all?'

'Perhaps not.' Lockie sighed. 'But he is here and you'll have to accept the fact that you'll be seeing him every now and then.'

'I seem to be falling over him every time I turn around,' Georgia exaggerated. 'Believe me, Lockie, where Jarrod's concerned I think the less we see of each other the better. Make no mistake, the feeling's mutual.'

'Is it?' Lockie asked quietly.

'It is.' Georgia was emphatic.

'Don't be too sure, Georgia. I'd say he's still carrying a pretty fair-sized torch for you.'

'That's ridiculous.' Georgia's words derided Lockie's opinion, while inside one tiny traitorous part of her rose up a tantalising wave of unadulterated hope. Could it be true? Did Jarrod…? No! Don't be a fool, she berated herself.

'Is it so ridiculous, Georgia? Then why does everything you say at him, and I mean *at* and not *to* him, pierce him down to bare bone?'

'What makes you think—?'

'Oh, come on, Georgia,' Lockie interrupted her. 'I've got eyes. I can tell when a bloke hangs on a girl's every word. And I've seen the knife-thrusts go home.'

'I've barely spoken to him.'

'I know. And that's the unkindest cut of all. Georgia, be honest with yourself. You're still in love with him and yet for some reason, heaven knows what—maybe guilt—you've decided to keep him dangling like a well-hooked fish on a line.'

Georgia stood up then, angrier with her brother than she'd been in years. 'That's absurd, Lockie. For a start I'm not still in love with him, and secondly, the guilt is definitely not mine. You don't know a thing about what happened so leave it alone.'

'I know more than—'

'You only think you know.' Georgia's voice rose and Lockie sighed.

'I just don't like to see two people I care about hurting— hurting themselves and each other.'

'I did all my hurting years ago. Now it's over. Finished.'

'Well, Jarrod's isn't.'

'That's his bad luck.'

'Georgia, give the bloke a break.'

'No, Lockie. I'm not going to let Jarrod, or anyone else for that matter, hurt me again,' Georgia said vehemently.

'Hurt you?' Lockie exclaimed. 'Good grief, Georgia! If he can forgive you—'

'Forgive me? For what?' Georgia broke in, her voice shrill.

'You should know for what. You don't need me to tell you.'

'Maybe I do need you to fill me in, Lockie, because I *don't* know. But apparently you think you do, so please enlighten me,' Georgia bit out with more than a touch of sarcasm.

'For two-timing him.'

'Two...' Georgia closed her mouth, her lips thinning. 'Did he tell you that?' she asked with ominous quietness.

If he had... Would Jarrod have twisted the truth so cruelly? She thought she'd reached the limit of the pain she'd had to endure, the pain Jarrod Maclean could put her through, but perhaps she hadn't.

'No, of course not,' Lockie denied. 'I didn't see Jarrod before he left for the States four years ago. I went over to tell him that you were...' He paused. 'That you had had an accident. Aunt Isabel told me Jarrod had gone and she didn't know where, and he wasn't coming back.

'There had to have been a pretty good reason for Jarrod to have gone off like that and I worked it out. You must have been seeing someone else, otherwise he'd never have left you—especially when...' His voice faded away and his eyes slid from hers.

'*I* had someone else?' Georgia asked bitterly, and her brother nodded. 'I don't suppose it occurred to you it might have been Jarrod who had someone else?'

Lockie met her hard gaze and slowly shook his head. 'No, Georgia. Jarrod worshipped you.'

Anger and pain rose inside Georgia until it almost choked her. Worshipped her? That was the joke of the century. If Lockie only knew. She sighed and just as suddenly her anger died. With a negating movement of her head she turned away from her brother, feeling ridiculously close to the tears she hadn't allowed to fall for years.

'Oh, Lockie. You couldn't be any further from the truth,' she said softly.

'I don't think I am, Georgia. Jarrod was in love with you and I thought you loved him.'

'You were half-right. I did. But he didn't!'

'Come on, Georgia. I was there too. I saw it all. I knew you went off to meet Jarrod, or at least I thought it was to meet him. But it wasn't, was it? There was another guy, wasn't there?' Lockie stepped closer to her. 'How could you do that to Jarrod, Georgia, when he loved you so much?'

She spun around to face him. 'There wasn't anyone else, Lockie; that's the truth. Not that it's any of your damn business, then or now.'

Lockie frowned. 'I can't believe you'd lie, Georgia. It's not like you. But I heard what you told Dad that night. I heard you say it wasn't Jarrod.'

Lockie had overheard! Georgia felt panic rise. She couldn't talk about that night. She wouldn't. It was far too agonising to remember, more than she would be able to bear.

'I don't want to discuss it, Lockie. I won't talk about it,' she finished, feeling hysteria rising and fighting it down.

'Georgia—'

'No, Lockie. Please.' Georgia held up her hand to halt their conversation. 'I've had enough. Now, just back off.'

She hurried past him and into her room, turning the key in the lock. A few minutes later she heard Lockie's door slam, and she sank tiredly onto her bed.

Georgia walked through the stock room of the bookshop, her nerveless fingers moving unconsciously on the strap of her shoulder bag.

'See you on Monday, Georgia.' Her workmate, Jodie, smiled a farewell. 'I'd say you'll be pleased to be going home; you've been a little distracted all day. Are you sure there isn't anything wrong?'

'No, Jodie, not exactly.' Georgia sighed. 'At least, nothing I can blame on anyone but myself.'

Jodie raised her eyebrows. 'Don't tell me.' She grinned. 'You allowed one of your family to talk you into something or other.'

'How did you guess?' Georgia gave a rueful laugh and Jodie's grin broadened.

'ESP. Or maybe you've just been wearing your ''worried about my family'' look all day.'

'It's not exactly the family. Well, indirectly. I'm afraid I've been a little more selfish than that. Today I've been whole-heartedly worried about myself.' Georgia glanced at her watch and swallowed the wave of nervous agitation that rose in her throat.

'Sounds ominous.' Jodie leant against her desk and folded her arms. 'You are going to tell me about it, aren't you? I mean, I can't stand the suspense.'

'Mandy's away and I've let Lockie talk me into taking her place and singing with his band tonight. I'm a mass of nerves just thinking about it. I don't know how I allowed him to do it but—well, I'm stuck with it now. Unless I develop a sudden virulent strain of laryngitis.' She pulled a face. 'But Lockie would never believe me.'

'Where will you be singing?'

'At the Country Music Club.'

Jodie straightened in surprise. 'In Ipswich?'

Georgia nodded and Jodie gave a low whistle.

'Wow! That's really something, Georgia. If I'd known I wouldn't have promised my parents I'd go over for dinner. I wonder if I can cry off? I'd love to hear you sing.'

'Oh, Jodie,' Georgia appealed. 'Don't make me feel more nervous than I am. I have this dreadful fear that I'll open my mouth and nothing will burst forth. Besides, you know you can't disappoint your parents.'

'I suppose not. But you'll be great, Georgia, and if I can I might be able to make it after dinner. What time do you go on?'

Georgia's brows drew together. 'I'm not sure of the exact time we start. They have a couple of guest artists as well. But we'll be on most of the night by the sound of it.' She glanced nervously at her wrist-watch again. 'I'd better go. Lockie's picking me up. But there's no need to go rushing up to Ipswich after work, Jodie, because the band's contracted for at least a month so there will be plenty of time to catch the show.'

And by then Lockie would have contacted Mandy and she would have flown back to Australia, she added to herself as she headed for the door.

'Georgia?' Jodie's voice had her pausing and turning back to face the other girl. 'Break a leg, OK?'

Georgia gave a wavering smile and continued out through the door.

Once outside the bookshop, she scanned the parking lot for Lockie's battered kombivan. As it wasn't there waiting she walked around to the front of the building to catch Lockie as he drove along the main street.

Five interminable minutes later there was still no sign of the van. Where was Lockie? Surely the kombi wouldn't choose today to break down again, would it? If Lockie was much longer she'd have to ring a taxi.

Nervously she paced the street, glancing again at her watch. She'd have to have some time, a little breathing-space, to sit down and calm herself before she had to take the stage. Otherwise she was going to let Lockie down by making a mammoth fool of herself.

The three practice sessions they'd had had gone really well considering, she tried to reassure herself, but her nervousness refused to heed her attempt at rationality.

Georgia groaned softly. Damn Lockie! Ever since they'd been children he'd managed to wheedle her into his wretched schemes. And always to her detriment. They'd always been caught out and now, with a surge of annoyed self-pity, Georgia

acknowledged that she had been the one on the receiving end
of the chastisement most of the time. Although Lockie was
older it seemed to be acceptable that he was a daredevil. She
was the sensible one so she should have had more sense.

Now she'd allowed Lockie to talk her into this—this nightmare. She could feel her knees tremble just at the thought of
the evening ahead. And if Lockie didn't put in an appearance
soon Georgia had the sneaking suspicion she'd either steal
spinelessly into the night or faint dead away right here on the
pavement.

A white station wagon drew to a halt in front of her and
the driver's door opened. The emblem on the side of the car
instantly removed what little composure she had left, and her
eyes flew panic-stricken to the man who climbed from behind
the wheel.

CHAPTER FIVE

'GEORGIA, come on. Get in,' his deep voice bade her as he stood half-in and half-out of the car.

Georgia was transfixed, standing stock-still, her thoughts swinging momentarily in limbo. She swallowed and unconsciously drew an uneven breath. What was *he* doing here?

'I'm illegally parked, Georgia. Do you want me to get a ticket?'

Like an activated puppet Georgia stepped mechanically towards the car and Jarrod subsided into the driver's seat to thrust open the passenger door from the inside.

'I'm waiting for Lockie.' Georgia's hand clutched the doorframe, and she made no move to climb in beside him. 'He'll be here any minute.'

'No, he won't. Lockie's van has a flat tyre so I offered to pick you up and drive you to the club,' he said shortly. 'Now, get in, Georgia.'

A car swung around the parked station wagon, tooting impatiently.

'Georgia, I'm going to create a traffic jam.'

Reluctantly she slid into the car, and with controlled movements Jarrod drove away.

'I thought it would be quicker for me to take you up to the club as Lockie's in the middle of setting up the sound and I don't suppose he'd want to take the time to change his tyre now.'

'Lockie never has time for the more mundane things like tyre-changing,' Georgia muttered, making a mental note to have stern words with her brother. They were falling into the habit of depending on Jarrod to come to their rescue when any plans came unstuck. Lockie had to realise that the less she saw of Jarrod, the better she'd like it. Hadn't she told him so?

'Lockie has the charm to get away with sidestepping those more mundane things.' There was a slight smiling tone in Jarrod's deep voice and the sound set Georgia's ragged nerve-ends shuddering with a wave of sudden, sharply bitter-sweet memory.

Angrily she pushed them aside. 'I'm sorry Lockie had to disturb you,' she began stiffly.

'I was coming up to the club anyway. And actually I'm glad he did ask me to give you a lift, as I want the opportunity to talk to you.'

Talk? Hadn't they said enough four years ago? Georgia wanted to throw the words out at him. 'And what exactly did you want to talk about?' she asked him succinctly.

'About you.'

'Me?' Georgia was too stunned to stop her voice squeaking. 'In what context?' she questioned as she got her breathing under control again.

'Lockie's band,' he said casually as he accelerated to join the traffic on the highway.

Georgia turned to gaze unseeingly at the passing scenery. Didn't he realise she was het up and nervous about tonight's performance? Surely Jarrod of all people would know how anxious she always was before she went on stage? He would remember... Why should he remember? she asked herself cruelly. If he had he wouldn't be trying to start an in-depth conversation with her now.

'What are you trying to say, Jarrod?' she asked flatly.

'I'm trying to say you'd be better off sticking with your job at the bookshop than trying to make a living at something as unpredictable as show business. It's all right for Lockie,' he continued. 'That's his bag. But it won't do for you, Georgia. I don't think you could cut that type of life.'

'Oh.' The anger began to build, pushing Georgia's nervous agitation to the back of her mind.

'And the singing, Georgia. Do you really enjoy it? I still say you weren't so keen in the old days.'

Don't, Jarrod! Don't talk about then. Not now, please, something inside her begged him. She just wanted to end this conversation. It might lead down a path she couldn't bear to travel with him.

'Would I be doing it if I didn't enjoy it?' she asked, not trying to hide the irritation in her voice.

'What about this demo tape Lockie wants to make? How do you feel about that?' Jarrod persisted, obviously not sensing her displeasure.

'That's all in Lockie's mind, just wishful thinking on his part at the moment. He can't afford it anyway.'

'He gave me to believe it's a distinct possibility. So are you interested?'

Georgia shrugged as he sent a sideways glance at her.

'Then why get involved in the band if you're not interested in this recording thing of Lockie's?' he asked flatly.

Quite honestly at that moment Georgia couldn't have cared less about Lockie's recording hopes. She just knew she was going to have a blazing row with her irresponsible brother in the very near future.

And as for her involvement in Lockie's plans—well, the sooner Mandy got back the better. Georgia was well aware she had her job at the bookshop and it was definitely more her style. But before she could admit this to Jarrod he was continuing his unwanted observations.

'The recording business isn't something you can do part-time. Lockie has plans for the band to do a national tour, and quite frankly I can't see flitting about the countryside suiting you, Georgia. Living out of suitcases. Hitting three towns every week. You said you were studying. What happens to that and your career then? Are you going to throw it away on the chance that the record will sell?'

Georgia's urge to demand why Jarrod thought any of this was his business warred with the sudden suspicion that perhaps her brother might have misled her again. Lockie hadn't mentioned Mandy's return since he'd convinced her to take the other girl's place. Had her brother really tried to contact Mandy? Or was he just going to expect her to stay on with the band after the weekend?

'I'm sure Lockie didn't say I was going to give up my job—' she began.

'The way Lockie's been talking, your job doesn't enter into the scheme of things.' He shifted exasperatedly in his seat. 'Be realistic, Georgia. How many home-grown records make the grade here in Australia? What security for your future is there in that?'

How dared he talk to her about security or her future when he'd brutally snatched that same security, that same future coolly, cruelly out from under her?

'Aren't you overreacting?' Georgia bit out between her clenched teeth. 'Lockie's a dreamer, you should know that. Even he would have to admit it. And this fellow Delaney he's been talking about—he may not even show up at the club. I can't see a man as busy as he must be hot-footing it into the sticks to check out a group of unknowns. I mean, this is the first decent engagement that Lockie's pulled off for Country Blues.'

Jarrod rubbed his hand along the line of his jaw, the sound rasping in the confines of the car. 'I just don't want to see you getting dragged along on Lockie's enthusiasm. Before you know it you could end up on a merry-go-round that won't and then can't stop.'

Why are you so worried about me now, Jarrod? Her inner self screamed at him and then challenged her. Ask him why? Why the interest at this late date? Was he so perturbed four years ago when he must have known he was breaking her heart? Ask him that.

'Why this sudden concern for my welfare?' The words tumbled from her lips.

'Sudden?' He raised an eyebrow as he pulled the car to a stop at a red light. 'Haven't I always been concerned? We've always been sort of family, after all, Georgia.'

'Family? Have we?' Her eyes met his and held them. 'And yes, I'd say sudden concern. You didn't find it necessary to be worried about me when—' her voice wavered slightly before she regained control of it '—when you were overseas.'

'Isabel kept me informed,' he said evenly, and Georgia gave a short laugh.

'Aunt Isabel did? We see Aunt Isabel once in three months or so under her sufferance. Even when I visited your father she was rarely there. She spends most of her time on the Gold Coast. What could she tell you about any of us? She's never shown any interest in Lockie, Morgan or me since we were born.'

Her interest was in you, Jarrod, she wanted to scream at him. Don't you remember?

She had always felt that relations between Jarrod and his stepmother had been uneasy, and as he'd grown older they had seemed to deteriorate. Or so she'd thought. In her naïvety she'd totally misinterpreted the situation until the night it had all fallen so agonisingly into place.

An undercurrent of volatile tension seemed to fill the car. Discussing her aunt, of all people, with Jarrod had the capacity to unlock a torrent of painful memories and she desperately forced them back before they took shape and cut her to the depths of her soul.

'I was in touch with Peter too,' Jarrod said flatly.

A brooding silence sat heavily upon them.

'Peter always told me how he enjoyed your visits,' Jarrod continued on a different note. 'He looked forward to you coming over to see him,' he added softly, and then that same shuttered look shrouded his face again.

'I enjoyed talking to him too,' Georgia conceded, wondering just how accurately Uncle Peter had reported their conversations over the past four years. There was hardly anything her uncle could have said anyway, for while Jarrod had been away they had talked about everything except her uncle's absent son.

'But we're getting away from the point.' Jarrod's words cut across Georgia's thoughts. 'And I can't drive and talk about this at the same time,' he said exasperatedly, and pulled off the road onto the verge, switching off the ignition and turning to face her.

Georgia glanced at her wrist-watch. 'Jarrod, I don't think we have time for this—' she began, and he moved one hand negatingly.

'A few minutes won't stop the show. All I intended to do was ensure you were aware of the pitfalls of the recording industry, and I'm speaking from firsthand experience.'

In her mind's eye Georgia had a fleeting glimpse of Jarrod all rigged out as a punk rocker, and a long-dormant spark of her old sense of humour struggled to the surface, taking her by surprise as her lips curved upwards at the corners and a soft, almost rusty chuckle escaped.

Jarrod's eyes appeared to be locked on her mouth and the muscles in his throat contracted as though he was having some difficulty drawing breath. The air between them crackled and Georgia's smile died.

Then Jarrod moved slightly, his hands adjusting the sash of his seat belt. His actions drew Georgia's attention to their nearness, to his taut, muscular thighs, the pale denim of his jeans not disguising the contours of his hard body, and it was her turn to fight for a steadying breath.

'What was so funny?' he was asking, seemingly unaware of the effect he had on her, had always had on her. And she must have imagined the tension that had momentarily seemed to hold him just as rigid as it had held her.

Georgia drew herself together. 'You said you had firsthand experience in the recording business. Why weren't we told you could sing?' Georgia raised her eyebrows enquiringly. 'Did you dye your hair purple and wear eye make-up?'

Jarrod blinked and then pulled a face. 'Not my own experience. A girl I knew in the States.'

A white-hot pain stabbed through Georgia as all her humour died, sliding back into the empty void of the last four years. So there had been girls. She'd have to be pretty naïve to imagine there hadn't been. Jarrod was a virile male, she knew that—knew just how potent he was from some firsthand experiences of her own. Yes, of course there would have been women.

'She was the sister of one of our engineers.' He was gazing into the distance. 'Her record took off and she couldn't handle the razzmatazz. She began with alcohol and then got into drugs.'

'Drugs?' Georgia stared at him incredulously. 'Don't you think that's going a bit far? I wouldn't know the first thing about the drug scene or where to find it.'

'It could find you, Georgia. I saw it happen to young Ginny.'

'This isn't Crime City, Jarrod. And give me more credit than that. Drugs would be no resort as far as I'm concerned, no matter how far down I fell.'

And I've already fallen down about as far as I can go, she added to herself. I fell right down when you pushed me, Jarrod Maclean. But I got up unaided.

'I'm sure young Ginny thought that way too. It was unbelievable, watching the change in her. As I said, I saw it firsthand.'

'Very close at hand by the sound of it.' Georgia's lips thinned, goaded by the thought of Jarrod and this unknown young American.

Jarrod's head went up and she felt his body stiffen. 'What's that supposed to mean?' he asked quietly.

She shrugged. 'Just that you seem to have had a close relationship with this girl.'

'I worked with her brother.'

Georgia shrugged again.

'She was just a kid. Eighteen or so.'

I was only seventeen when I fell for you, Jarrod. Or have you so very conveniently forgotten? Georgia's eyes met, held and told his, and his lips tightened.

'I met Ginny socially through her brother, that's all.'

Georgia continued to gaze at him, unaware of the accusation in her eyes, and Jarrod swore, running a hand through his hair. One lock fell forward onto his brow, thoroughly distracting Georgia, making her want to reach out, smooth it back, feel the silken texture once again.

'For heaven's sake, Georgia, why am I trying to explain this to you?' he asked, clipping the words out.

'Why, indeed?' She was inciting him with uncharacteristic spite, his words pushing her, driving her, while part of her shrank inside with horror at her behaviour.

'Look, I'm just trying to illustrate a point I'm making about the music scene, and whether I took the girl to bed or not doesn't enter into it.'

'And did you?'

He gazed at her stormily. 'Did I what?' he voiced unnecessarily.

'Take her to bed.' Georgia persisted through suddenly dry, inflexible lips. My God! Why had she asked him that? Where was her pride?

'Would it make any difference if I had?' he bit out angrily.

Georgia's gaze fell, her lashes shielding the agony his words evoked, pain she knew would be reflected in their dark depths. Not to you, Jarrod. But all the world to me, her heart cried out inside her.

Jarrod sighed loudly and muttered an imprecation. 'My relationship with Ginny is totally irrelevant. And this conversation's beginning to get to me. All I wanted to say, Georgia, was that this dream of Lockie's may not be what you want to do with your life.'

'Aren't you surmising rather a lot, Jarrod? How would you know what I want to do with my life?'

'I just know you, Georgia, and—'

'You know me?' Georgia broke in on him with a sharp, exaggerated laugh and he frowned. 'Do you know me, Jarrod? Or do you only think you do? And know in what context?' she added suggestively, wanting to provoke him but perversely feeling no sense of success when a slight flush coloured the line of his cheekbones. She could tell she was getting to him but just what was she achieving?

'You never used to be like this, Georgia.' His voice was soft, a little uneven.

Bring this conversation to an end, she warned herself. She had to finish it now, before her inflaming words betrayed her, but she couldn't do it, and she suspected she had somehow lost control of herself. 'Like what?'

'Bitter. Hostile.'

Oh, Jarrod. Her broken heart yearned to scream at him, wound him, lay his feelings as bare as he'd exposed hers. Yes, she was bitter. And she knew she was hostile. But she was still hurting. Because of him. Yet, after all this time, after all he'd done, when he was cut, she bled.

'Perhaps it's old age.' A wave of weary resignation washed the conflict out of her. 'And a little cynicism. We all change with life's experiences, don't we? So there's no need for you to concern yourself, Jarrod. I shan't fall by the wayside like your little girlfriend in the States.'

'Ginny wasn't my girlfriend—' He stopped and swore under his breath, his hands gripping the steering wheel, his body tense with emotion.

Anger, Georgia recognised. But there was something else— something that drew a spontaneous, involuntary response deep inside her—and she was unable to prevent herself moving back in her seat.

'So you said.'

'And you never used to be a bitch, Georgia.'

'Maybe that's something else experience has taught me,' she got out, and at his expression her hand came up between them as though to ward him off. 'All right. This Ginny was your girl—space—friend.' Georgia's body was pressing back against the seat as she forced herself as far away from the totally disturbing nearness of his hard body as the close confines of the car would allow.

Then, to her horror, of its own accord, her hand fell to rest on his shirt front, the feel of the body-warmed material beneath her fingers burning, searing. Yet she was incapable of drawing away, sybaritic fascination seemingly outweighing the pain of touching him again. And she couldn't breathe. Her lungs refused to draw breath. Her heartbeats thundered, surging in her ears in a deafening crescendo.

For what seemed to Georgia like a lifetime they sat like that, neither moving, held in some unseen emotional thrall, until Jarrod's own hand came up to cover hers. For a split second his fingertips were a caress, pure and agonising, before she snatched her hand away from his and clutched her fingers together in her lap.

'Georgia.'

The word was torn from him and she tried to tell herself that she should be glad she'd finally succeeded in pushing him to the edge, that she should rejoice. But she could only quiver inside with fear—fear that she was playing too close to the fire, that her emotions were tinder-dry and just one spark might unleash the embers of the passion they had once shared.

She heard the breath he'd been holding whistle softly through his teeth and knew his eyes were boring down on the top of her bent head. With a muttered oath he reached out and flicked on the ignition, the roar of the engine rasping on Georgia's still sensitive nerve-endings.

'We'd better get a move on,' he said flatly. 'You have a show to do.'

They rejoined the traffic flow, completing the remainder of their journey in a heavy, totally unnerving silence. As they

pulled into the car park Lockie's van was still resting lopsid-
edly on its flat tyre and they barely had time to climb from
the car before Morgan came running towards them.

'Thank goodness you're here, Georgia. Lockie's been beside himself waiting for you. I think he thought Jarrod had
run off with you.' She turned to Jarrod with a cheeky grin,
her eyes flashing flirtatiously.

'We go on in less than half an hour,' Georgia reminded
them shortly, and began walking towards the entertainers' en-
trance.

'You don't say!' Morgan exclaimed sarcastically. 'And
there's no time to waste, Georgia. At your age you'll need
every minute to put on your make-up.' She turned back to
Jarrod. 'Anyone would think she was the rock of ages the way
she goes on.'

They walked along a short passageway until Morgan
stopped.

'Go on through there, Jarrod.' She directed him, unaware
of the band of tension that arced between the other two.
'They've saved us a table in front. I'll join you when I've
helped Georgia with her costume.'

With one sombre glance at Georgia Jarrod left them, and
with no little difficulty Georgia forced the portentous scene in
the car from her mind.

In a daze she struggled out of her suit jacket and skirt and
into the emerald-green costume that Mandy usually wore.

'How's the top?' Morgan asked as Georgia's nervous fingers fumbled with the buttons. 'I tried to let it out as far as I
could, like you said.'

Georgia straightened the emerald-green satin shirt and the
row of white fringing shimmered from the long fitting sleeves.
'It's not exactly made to measure, is it?' She grimaced, wondering if she had the nerve to leave the small dressing room
wearing it.

Morgan gave an irritated sigh. 'Well, you are a little more
well endowed than Mandy, Georgia. Just don't make any sud-

den movements, like throwing your arms wide. Otherwise we could be trampled under foot as the guys in the audience stampede for the stage.'

'Morgan, please.' Georgia groaned, smoothing the blouse over her midriff. The matching skirt hugged her hips and could have been made for her, but the top was another story. The soft, sleek material clung to the rounded fullness of her breasts a little too snugly for Georgia's liking. She glanced at her reflection in the long mirror behind the door and decided that that was a mistake.

Hurriedly she applied a little make-up—dark mascara to emphasise her long lashes, blusher to highlight her cheekbones and bring some colour to her pale face, and a soft lipgloss following the curve of her full lips. The face looking back at her made her feel that she was looking at someone she hadn't seen for a long, long time.

It made her realise just how little attention she'd been giving her appearance over the last four years. Oh, she had always been neat and tidy, but the Georgia Grayson who gazed at her from the mirror was so alive somehow. Her eyes sparkled. Her lips trembled slightly. And her dark hair, unconfined at her nape, fell in soft waves to her shoulders.

She drew a steadying breath, drawing her attention to the figure-hugging blouse once more. The loose, subdued clothes she wore to work barely hinted at the fullness of her breasts, her narrow waist.

'Oh, Morgan, I can't wear this.'

'Rubbish! You look sensational, Georgia. You'll have all the guys drooling. In fact—' Morgan put her head on the side, regarding her sister '—it always amazes me that you haven't got a whole tribe of men knocking down the door.'

Georgia winced. 'If that's a compliment, thanks. But sorry, I'm not interested,' she added wryly.

'Pigs you're not interested. Gee! You're such a pain, Georgia.' Morgan struck a pose in the doorway. 'Sometimes

I could shake you. Anyone would think you were fifty. Talk about a crusty old maid locked up in a bookshop.'

Georgia flushed. Crusty, maybe. But old maid? No, she couldn't in all honesty lay claim to that description. 'Please don't talk like that, Morgan. I find it offensive,' she chastised her. 'Why must you always be so personal?'

'I just say what I think. I'm honest.'

'There's a fine line between honesty and rudeness.'

'Oh, spare me, big sister. And sometimes the truth hurts. Do you know who you remind me of?' Morgan challenged. 'Aunt Isabel. All cool and icy and withdrawn. You never have any fun. What do you do with your time? Go to work. Study. And you never laugh. It must be like wearing a strait-laced corset. You're forever telling me what to do but at least I'm living; I'm getting out and tasting life.'

Tasting life. Georgia took the words like a blow. If Morgan only knew. Georgia had tasted all of life she wanted to sample. Perhaps she had sated herself on it, for it had left her sick to her stomach.

Morgan let out an exasperated breath. 'OK. I'm sorry. But you don't always bring out the best in me, Georgia, and I guess this isn't the time and place. We should get out there.'

Georgia stifled a slightly hysterical cross between a groan and a giggle. 'I'm a fool for letting Lockie talk me into this,' she muttered, rubbing her cold hands together.

'There's no need to be nervous,' Morgan said, her tone a little less antagonistic. 'The rehearsal last night went great. If you sing half as well tonight you'll be an instant success.'

'I wish,' Georgia murmured.

Morgan grinned and went to leave her. She paused and turned back to her sister. 'Oh, and Georgia, don't worry.' She indicated the emerald-green blouse. 'Dolly Parton's record may have been rocked slightly but it still stands.'

Before Georgia could comment Morgan had disappeared and the music began. Georgia bit her lip and moaned. Country Blues was playing its introductory number, a fast instrumental.

After that the boys would do a short set of John Denver numbers and then Lockie was going to introduce Georgia. It was time for her to go into the wings and await her cue.

Cool. Icy. Humourless. Withdrawn. An old maid afraid to face life. Had Morgan really said all that? The young girl didn't know how cruel she had been in her ignorance. Only four short years ago all those adjectives would have been the exact opposite of Georgia Grayson.

Jarrod's face swam before her, his eyes dark with a heavy sensuality that had matched her own... Just four short years ago.

The rumble of applause vibrated, the sound deafening to Georgia as she stood waiting, her heart in her mouth. The audience had appreciated the opening songs. Now Lockie was introducing the individual members of the band. In moments she would have to go out on stage. In front of the sea of faces. Including Jarrod.

He disapproved of her singing tonight. Yet he had no right to that criticism. No rights over her at all. She straightened her spine and then remembered the buttons on her shirt. She fingered them nervously.

'So please welcome the pretty face of Country Blues. Georgia Grayson.' Lockie's voice over the microphone sank into her consciousness and Georgia stepped shakily forward, making her rubbery legs carry her onto the stage.

The heat of the lights hit her and she almost gasped. The audience was cheering, wolf-whistles rising above the general clapping as the band struck up Georgia's opening number. Grab them with a fast, jazzy one, Lockie had said, then we'll slay them with a tear-jerker.

Trying not to single out anyone in particular in the crowd of dimly lit faces below, Georgia took the mike from its stand. But of course her eyes found Jarrod immediately. She had always had built-in radar where he was concerned.

He sat back in his seat, arms folded, unsmiling.

Did he think she would fail? Well, she wasn't going to make

a fool of herself or the boys. She *could* sing and she'd show Jarrod Maclean just how talented she was.

By the time she was halfway through the song she knew the audience was with her and the feeling elated her, carried her on, gave her a heady power. She shot Lockie a quick glance and he beamed at her, his eyes saying, I told you so!

Now for the change of pace. She led into the romantic, almost melancholy lyrics and her eyes returned of their own accord to Jarrod. He was sitting forward now, a tension in him, and she felt his eyes burning on her.

The catch in her voice was real, and the throb of unrequited love was a web she spun. The listeners felt it slip around each one of them but at that moment Georgia saw only one dark head, one craggy face. Only one. It had always been that way for her. She had loved him once. So very much. Before she'd learned the truth about him.

She could see quite clearly in that moment of vivid recall the living room at the Maclean house. She had been at the Macleans' that evening as usual and she and Jarrod had sat watching television together. Uncle Peter had been away on business and even the slightly disapproving presence of Aunt Isabel hadn't been able to dim Georgia's happiness just being with Jarrod.

At about nine-thirty Aunt Isabel had pointedly made supper—coffee and her famous shortbread—and she'd reminded Jarrod he had to be up early to collect his father from the airport.

Georgia could see him now as he turned to her, smiling crookedly at his stepmother's pointed comments.

'Come on, I'll walk you home.'

'It would be quicker to take the car,' her aunt put in drily. 'It's late enough as it is.'

'Oh, no. It's not so late,' Georgia said quickly, clutching at the opportunity to have Jarrod to herself. 'And it's such a lovely moonlit night I intended to walk home anyway.' She glanced imploringly at Jarrod and he smiled.

'OK. Let's go.' He slipped his arm around Georgia's shoulder. ''I won't be long, Isabel, but you go on to bed. I have my key.'

They walked together in silence, Jarrod's arm now lightly around her waist, and a wild, inexplicable joy raced along Georgia's veins as his long body brushed hers as they moved. And she could feel with burning intensity the imprint of his fingers through her thin cotton top.

'Just look at that moon, Jarrod.' Her heart swelled and she knew the moon's beauty had little to do with it.

'You can almost discern colours by it,' he replied. 'No fear of falling in a ditch; it's just about daylight.'

Georgia swallowed. Did Jarrod feel the fire where they touched? How she wished she lived miles further away so that these moments could be prolonged.

They came to the fork in the track and Georgia stopped when he went to veer to the right.

'Let's go over the creek and up the hill.' It was shorter, through the bush and away from the road, but, to Georgia, so much more romantic. 'I'll bet the view in the moonlight is unreal.'

'Georgia, I've told you that the bridge isn't safe. The timber's rotting, it's so old.'

'I know. But we'll be careful. Come on, Jarrod. Please?'

He sighed exasperatedly and shook his head. 'I never seem to be able to refuse you anything, do I? You flash those big brown eyes at me and I'm putty in your hands.'

'Really?' Georgia chuckled. 'Now I know that deep dark secret of yours my life's complete.'

Jarrod kissed the tip of her nose and wrapped an arm about her waist again as they walked on along the well-moonlit track. And Georgia felt a rush of pure happiness. Her life was complete. She had Jarrod's love and everything was wonderful.

When they reached the bridge Jarrod gingerly led the way across the creaking timbers and, once on the other side, he turned to help her off the last step onto the path. Georgia slid into his arms and drew in the heady scent of him. Remnants of his musky aftershave. The clean freshness of his soft cotton shirt. The essence that was totally him.

This was their favourite spot. They often climbed the bank, sat beneath the concealing overhang of the scrubby trees, talked for hours, kissed.

'Let's go up the bank,' Georgia whispered, her heartbeats hammering in unison with the heavy thud of his.

Jarrod glanced upwards. 'It's late. I should be getting you home.'

Georgia heard the slight edge of indecision in his voice and knew he wanted to hold her close. She took his hand and started up the bank, pulling him after her. And he didn't resist.

The dry leaves on the trees overhead barely stirred as he drew her into his arms, kissing her gently before pulling slightly back from her.

'What was I saying about not being able to deny you anything?' he murmured wryly, his fingertips rubbing the soft skin at the base of her throat.

'It's the same for me.' She swallowed thickly. 'Oh, Jarrod, touch me.'

CHAPTER SIX

His arms tightened and his lips found hers. In moments the kiss had deepened and their bodies strained urgently, moulding together.

A shaft of wanting shot to the pit of Georgia's stomach to explode in a starburst of desire. She could feel the hardness of Jarrod's arousal too, and sensed the subtle change in the tension that held him. Then they sank down onto the sandy earth, their hands insistently exploring each other's bodies.

Georgia's fingers pulled at the buttons of Jarrod's shirt, slipped it back from his shoulders, and her lips trailed over the smooth, silken contours of his shoulders, his chest, his hard, flat midriff. The moonlight filtering through the dry leaves kissed him too and Georgia caught her breath.

'You're beautiful,' she murmured, her voice thick.

His low, throaty laugh cascaded over her and he lifted her loose cotton top over her head, unclipped her bra, feeling her full breasts. 'I'm beautiful? You're the beautiful one,' he whispered, and his lips went to her breasts, his tongue-tip teasing first one hardening rosy peak and then the other.

Georgia rested backwards, her arms supporting her, her fingers curling into the warm sand, and she closed her eyes. The craving in her body intensified, flowed through her to her fingertips, the very tips of her toes.

His lips left her breast, slid upwards over her throat, her chin, found her mouth again, kissing her druggingly. When they drew apart they were both breathless.

Jarrod reached for his shirt and when Georgia would have

protested, begged him not to put it back on he spread it behind her and gently laid her back onto the ground, his lips caressing her again.

His touch tantalised her body, caressed her breasts, fingers unbuttoned her skirt, circled her navel, moved downwards before sliding upwards over the smooth skin of her thigh, to find her most responsive core. She arched against him, the breath of her husky, incited moan teasing his sensitive ear lobe. Jarrod tensed and she felt him pause, sensed he was going to put some cooling space between them.

'No!' Georgia cried thickly. 'Please, Jarrod. Don't stop.'

Her hand covered his and then moved to the press stud on his jeans. It sprang open, the noise crashing into the stillness of the moonlit night. She drew down his zipper, her fingers finding him, exciting him the way he was exciting her, and he groaned in concession. Seconds or hours later they were naked, bodies entwined.

One small part of Georgia acknowledged that they were both way past being capable of drawing back but she knew she didn't care. She loved Jarrod so much and he loved her. If the earth had chosen that moment to disintegrate she wouldn't have noticed.

Then Jarrod's glistening body moved over her, settled into her, and their smooth, slick skin slid together. And the earth did explode. She cried out into the salty dampness of Jarrod's shoulder as waves of pleasurable release washed over her.

The applause swelled in the well-known club as the patrons rose to their feet. Georgia came back to earth slowly, acknowledging their accolades with a shy smile that hid a sudden wave of cynicism. Why *wouldn't* she be able to give the poignant lyrics life? The sad lament could have been written for her. And Jarrod.

She moved back to allow Lockie centre stage. In this set she would only be called upon to harmonise in the chorus.

She would have staked her life on Jarrod's integrity back

then. But it appeared that the man she'd fallen in love with
and the real Jarrod Maclean were worlds apart. And the pain
engendered by his perfidy still gripped her now, was as real
as it had been during the many hours she'd spent waiting for
him to come back to her.

But she'd eventually pulled herself out of that black abyss
of despair, out and over the top of it. Her Jarrod Maclean and
the small part of himself he had given her were lost to her for
ever, would never return. She'd learned to live with that.

Then why did this hurting remain?

Georgia brushed her hair impatiently back from her face.
When you'd loved with the intensity that she had loved it took
time to get over it.

Four years? she taunted herself relentlessly.

The whole and only cause of this morbid wallow into the
past was Jarrod's reappearance. He'd turned up like the pro-
verbial bad penny and he was throwing her calm, relatively
ordered life into disarray, making her remember things she'd
put behind her, proving so easily that her past wasn't as deeply
entombed as she had imagined it to be.

But you'll never be so young, so full of life, of love. Forget
it, Georgia, she reproached herself. Forget Jarrod and what he
did. He's only here for a brief stay to comfort his dying father.
And when Uncle Peter loses his so precarious hold on life
then Jarrod will leave again. Just keep out of his way, and
keep him out of your mind.

Besides, until those moments in the car this evening he
hadn't really shown any sign that he wanted to remember the
intimacies they'd shared. She was probably only one of his
many memories, hazily forgotten.

And he certainly hadn't given the impression he wanted to
take up where they'd left off. Not that Georgia wanted to. It
was ludicrous even to think about it. She might still find him
physically attractive but as a man she hated him, could never
forgive him.

Yet of their own accord her eyes sought him out. He was

leaning towards Morgan, apparently trying to catch what the young girl was saying above the sound of the music.

Georgia had never felt that there was more than a very slight family resemblance between herself and her young sister, but from her position on the stage she could have been looking down on herself.

Morgan's young face glowed as her bright eyes so obviously admired Jarrod's chiselled features. And her hand rested companionably on his arm as she leant closer, her mouth within a mere inch of his ear.

What was Morgan saying? Whatever it was, Jarrod's lips moved upward at the corners in amusement. He'd smiled at Georgia in that same affectionate way as she'd grown up. Surely Jarrod wasn't interested in Morgan? Her blood ran cold. No! Morgan was only seventeen, barely more than a child. He wouldn't... She forced herself to drag her eyes from the cosy cameo they made.

The hours flew by and the audience didn't want them to stop playing. They stomped for encore after encore and when Georgia finally left the stage and reached the dressing room she sank down on the chair totally exhausted.

The tiny dressing room filled with a crush of people, eyes all glowing, congratulatory. Lockie and the boys were kissing her; even Morgan was smiling. And through a break in the faces, leaning solidly against the doorjamb, was Jarrod.

Georgia's bright eyes met his and his lips twisted in a crooked half-smile. He inclined his head in unspoken acknowledgement.

Very magnanimous, Jarrod, her silent regard flashed at him. Did he think she needed his approbation? She turned swiftly, brutally away from him.

When the last patron had finally left the club and Lockie and the boys had switched off all their equipment they sat around the now silent stage drinking coffee, all a little loath to bring the night to an end.

Georgia had changed back into her own clothes and removed her make-up. It had been too much trouble to put her hair back into its confining band so she'd left it loose about her shoulders, unaware that the softness of the style drew attention to the shape of her face, giving it a youthful, ethereal beauty.

Jarrod sat at a table just slightly apart from them all, slowly drinking his coffee. After one quick, inscrutable glance at Georgia as she joined them he kept his attention on the cup in his hand.

'Here comes our star.' Lockie grinned.

'Don't be silly, Lockie. One night does not a star make,' Georgia misquoted a little breathily. Some of her euphoria had dissipated with the removal of her costume and make-up and she was suddenly bone-weary.

'Have it your way, Georgia.' Lockie sighed exasperatedly. 'But perhaps you'll believe me when I tell you the owner of the club is more than pleased with our show.'

Georgia raised her eyebrows.

'And,' Lockie continued, 'there were some people here with a good bit of clout in the industry and I have it on good authority they were impressed—that's with a capital I.' He sprang to his feet and danced a jig. 'We're in! We're in! After all this time. In the old days, didn't I tell you I'd make it one day, Jarrod?' He turned to the other man.

'At least once a week.' Jarrod smiled drily.

Lockie feigned a punch in his direction and subsided onto a table-top, raising his eyes skywards. 'Oh, boy! I can't wait till Sunday so I can phone Mandy. Have I dreamed of this moment? We all have, haven't we, guys?'

'And what about you, Georgia?' asked Evan Green, the guitarist, after they'd all laughingly agreed with Lockie. 'Has tonight made all your dreams come true too?'

Georgia tensed as a shaft of pain tore through her. Dreams. What were they? Transient things at best. Pure torture at their worst. Any dreams she'd had were dreams of loving, marrying, having children, growing old together—together with

Jarrod. And they'd been smashed. Jarrod had sliced them apart in those few short destructive moments four years ago. Since then dreams had had no part in her life. Dreams were luxuries she wouldn't allow herself to indulge in again.

She shrugged. 'Let's not get too carried away on the wings of one night's success,' she said flatly.

'Good grief! What a crashing bore you are, Georgia.' Morgan grimaced as she crossed to sit at the table with Jarrod. 'Now don't try to tell us you didn't enjoy this evening. I saw your eyes sparkling. Must have been all those guys gazing up at you in total admiration.'

'Admiration?' Andy put his large arm around Georgia's shoulders. 'Now that's a new word for it. Wait until tomorrow night after word has got around. We'll have our hands full fighting off the guys, Lockie; you mark my words.'

Georgia flushed and pushed herself gently away from the solidity of Andy's body. 'And who says I'll want you to fight them off?'

'Shouldn't we be heading off home now?' Jarrod's deep voice broke in on the loud guffaws and Georgia's gaze swung to him.

He was standing now, feet apart, and she recognised that particular tilt of his jaw. It unleashed another flashback with equally acute clarity.

She had been singing with Lockie's band at the local primary-school reunion and Jarrod had been in the audience, as he had been tonight. After her initial nervousness Georgia had known she'd performed well and everyone had sought her out to congratulate her. Yet Jarrod had said nothing. Until they were driving home.

'It was a lovely day, wasn't it?' she began, glancing uncertainly at him, trying to think of an explanation for his silence.

'And, just think,' she rushed on, 'old Mrs Kruger and Mr Jones enrolled at the school when it was first opened seventy-five years ago. They didn't look that old, did they?' She slid along the bench seat, closer to Jarrod's hard body. 'Do you suppose we'll go back too, in, say, another fifty years?'

He half smiled then. 'You probably will, Georgia, but I can't see myself lasting the distance. You're younger than I am.'

A cloud passed over her face and her fingers tightened when they rested on his thigh. 'Not that much younger, Jarrod. And I want to grow old with you,' she added softly, seriously.

Jarrod took one hand off the steering wheel and covered her hand, lacing his fingers through hers. Then he'd sung a few bars of the Beatles' song, 'When I'm Sixty-Four', making her laugh again.

'You'll be the prettiest, sexiest sixty-four-year-old lady in town,' he said, raising her hand to his lips and kissing it gently.

'Oh, Jarrod.' She rested her head on his shoulder. 'I'm glad you're in a good mood again. Why have you been so quiet?'

'Quiet? Have I?'

'You know you have. What was the matter?'

He sighed. 'The day. The past. I guess I felt "old" creeping up on me. And hearing you sing, seeing you up there on the stage, watching the audience watching you—it made me realise just how talented you are. I suppose I was jealous.'

'Jealous?' Georgia dimpled and he grimaced.

'I didn't like having to share you with all those other people. Especially the guys,' he added self-derisively.

'But I was singing to you,' Georgia said softly, her voice thick with her need to kiss him, hold him close.

Jarrod slowed the car and turned into a little-used gravel lay-by. He stopped and pulled her urgently into his arms.

'All my songs are for you,' Georgia whispered, lifting her face eagerly for his kiss, meeting him with reciprocal passion.

'And I'm selfish enough to want them to be for me alone,' he groaned as his lips found hers.

Now Georgia blinked the vivid scene from her mind. It could have been yesterday. The situations were practically the same. She had been on the stage and Jarrod part of the audience. She'd sung love songs just for him and his eyes had darkened with jealousy. The way his eyes had darkened again tonight.

In that moment of recall, hope burst forth inside her like new shoots after rain, blossoming in a vertiginous ascension that briefly deprived her of breath. Jarrod was jealous. Tonight. As he had been all those years ago. Then in a sobering rush she remembered.

And with that recollection came the terrible, almost unbearable sensations of loss. Her heart constricted painfully in her chest and she unconsciously clutched at Andy's arm so tightly that he turned to her full of concern.

'Georgia?' He frowned worriedly. 'What is it?'

'Nothing. Sorry.' She took a deep breath, striving to regain her self-possession. 'I'm just tired, I guess. I've been up on a high and my body's telling me it's time to come down to earth.'

Lockie's quick glance slid from his sister's pale face to Jarrod and he stepped forward. 'Yes, we should be going. We all need our beauty sleep.' He gave Andy a slap on the back. 'Some of us more than others.'

'Very funny!' exclaimed Andy drily.

'Hey, how are you getting home, Lockie?' Ken asked. 'I thought you didn't have a spare tyre to put on the van.'

'I'll leave the van here overnight. Andy and Evan can go with you and we'll go with Jarrod.' He grinned at the other man. 'You won't mind dropping us off, will you, mate?'

Jarrod shook his head and Morgan patted his arm. 'Again! They'll have you in the taxi drivers' union before you know it, Jarrod.' She looked up at him. 'How did we manage before you came home?'

We managed, Morgan, Georgia wanted to cry out. And we could have managed now if Lockie had simply ordered a cab. They didn't need Jarrod.

But her eyes were drawn to him, had him in profile, his dark hair neatly styled, cropped short in the front, the thick, vital strands almost reaching his collar at the back. He was unbelievably, even unfairly attractive, his deep chest narrowing to his lean waist and hips, his jeans moulding the athletic length of his legs.

For heaven's sake, she chided herself. She seemed to have developed a fixation on his body. She couldn't seem to prevent her eyes from devouring him. Was this what not being able to touch him was doing to her?

Pull yourself together, Georgia Grayson, she silently commanded herself with bitter self-contempt. If she kept leering at him everyone would begin to notice. And begin to wonder...

'Come on, Georgia. Have you fallen asleep on your feet?' Lockie brought her out of her censorious reverie and she hurried after them.

Walking into the kitchen, Georgia stood the empty laundry basket in its place behind the door and swept her tangled hair back from her face. She had finished hanging out their washing and the gusty wind would ensure that it would soon be dry.

Morgan intended to take the bus down to the shopping centre to meet her friends but Lockie had been dead to the world when the girls had had their breakfast.

'Is Lockie still in bed?' Georgia asked now, as Morgan passed her a cup of coffee.

'I called him again half an hour ago but there aren't any signs of life from his side of the house as yet.'

Georgia shook her head. 'He should be setting off to pick up his flat tyre soon. The tyre centre will be closed if he doesn't.'

'He's pretty slack, isn't he? Lazy devil.' Morgan made a face. 'If it hadn't been for Jarrod who knows how we'd have got home last night?'

'We'd have taken a taxi,' Georgia replied drily, and took a sip of her tea. 'Morgan,' she began, 'about Jarrod...'

Morgan looked up and smiled broadly. 'What about him? Wow! Isn't he a turn on? I could really go for him in a big way.'

'He's nearly old enough to be your father.' The ridiculous words were out before Georgia could draw them back. And she'd promised herself she was going to be tactful.

'Am I glad he isn't!' Morgan laughed.

'Well, he is a little too old, too experienced for you—'

'Oh, no!' Morgan broke in, her good humour fading. 'Not another lecture! Save it, Georgia.' She put her hands on her hips. 'You had your chance with him and you blew it, so if I want a turn you're not going to stop me.'

Georgia bit her lip in the horror she could barely hide. 'I didn't mean—'

'All's fair, Georgia, so lay off.'

Georgia flushed and Morgan threw her hands in the air.

'Who says I'm interested in him anyway? I'm only having a bit of fun. And I'm all grown up so you don't have to warn me about the big bad wolf.'

'I didn't intend... I mean...'

'Oh, good grief!' Morgan raised her hands and let them fall. 'Don't put yourself through this, Georgia. Look,' she enunciated deliberately, 'Jarrod's no more interested in me than I am in him. He's all yours, big sister, but take a tip from me. Don't leave him hanging too long. There are plenty of females out there who won't stand in line.'

'Morgan, I have no intention of vying for any man's attention.'

Morgan rolled her eyes exasperatedly. 'We shouldn't let you out alone, Georgie. And having you on is beginning to be no fun at all. You're far too gullible.'

'I'm not—' Georgia stopped and sighed. Why did Morgan have this knack of putting her on the wrong foot all the time? 'Let's just change the subject. Did he...did Jarrod mention the job that may be available at the Ipswich office?'

'Yes.'

Georgia's heart sank at the monosyllabic reply. 'Do you think you might be interested?'

'I guess.' Morgan shrugged. 'Jarrod said I'd have to do a basic word-processing course and maybe one on office skills.'

'It sounds ideal,' Georgia began gently, not wanting to put her sister off the idea.

'I'm going to think about it,' was all Morgan would say.

'Oh-h-h!' A deep groan interrupted them, heralding Lockie's groggy entry into the kitchen. 'Who set the time bombs going off in my head?'

Morgan turned to face her brother. 'Don't complain to us, Lockie. Nobody forced you to have that champagne when we got home last night. You know what it does to you so you won't get any sympathy here.'

Georgia pulled herself together as Lockie groped his way to the table. When they'd finally arrived home in the early hours of the morning Lockie had insisted on opening the bottle of champagne one of the patrons had left for them, but he had been the only one to take more than an obligatory sip.

'I have to have coffee. Lots of it.' He gingerly lowered his lanky frame into a chair. 'At least you'll have mercy, won't you, Georgia?'

Silently Georgia set a cup of strong black coffee in front of him, the pottery mug clunking on the bare wooden table-top.

Lockie flinched. 'Ouch! What was that explosion? Has my head fallen off?'

'It would have to have something in it to fall off,' Morgan remarked. 'More likely to blow away in the breeze.'

Georgia laughed softly and patted his shoulder. 'Be sure your sins have caught up with you, Lockie Grayson.'

He grimaced and took a gulp of coffee. 'Ah.' He sighed. 'Lovely. I may be saved.'

'You'd better save yourself pretty quickly. The tyre centre will be closing in a couple of hours,' Georgia reminded him.

'Yes, and Jarrod will be wondering where you are,' Morgan

added. 'You said you were going to borrow his car early this morning.'

Lockie glanced bleary-eyed at the kitchen clock. 'Is it that late? Ugh! I need a shower before I can drive anywhere. How about popping over and picking up Jarrod's car for me, Morgan?'

'No way, brother dear. I've made other plans and I'm just about to leave.' She picked up her bag. 'You'll have to collect it yourself or coerce Georgia into doing it for you.'

Lockie shot a look at his other sister. 'How about it, Georgia?'

'Really, Lockie! It's about time you learned some sense of responsibility.' Georgia frowned in irritation.

'Amen,' agreed Morgan.

'Are you two ganging up on a sick man?'

'All your own fault,' was Morgan's parting remark.

Turning to Georgia, Lockie put on his most beguiling expression. 'Could you pick up Jarrod's car while I shower and change?'

'Oh, Lockie,' she began. She had no desire to cross Jarrod's path again so soon. As it was, his face as he'd gazed up at her on the stage had kept her sleepless for some time when she'd finally got to bed after the show.

'He probably won't be there, Georgia,' Lockie said quietly, and her eyes flew to meet her brother's before sliding away. 'I think he said he was going into the office this morning.'

Georgia moved restlessly over to the sink and made a big job of rinsing her cup. And which was worse? she upbraided herself. Seeing him or not seeing him?

She heard Lockie sigh.

'It's OK, Georgia. I'll collect the car myself.' He stood up.

'No. Have your shower, Lockie.' Georgia walked over to the door. 'I'll go. I could do with the walk over there. I won't be long.'

'You're a pal, Georgia.' Lockie grinned and she pulled a face at him.

Georgia headed out through the front gate. She could have taken the path through the gate in the back fence—it was the shortest route to the Macleans'—but she hadn't been that way in years.

For months after that dreadful time of Jarrod's betrayal she had haunted the much trodden track through the scrubby bushland and long, dry grass, up the low, knobby hill, by the usually waterless creek bed. Up the bank and under the trees.

But then she'd come to her senses, realised the folly of her youthful, trusting love. What would she achieve by putting herself through the pain, by reliving the agony? It was self-destructive and she'd decided she wasn't going to allow Jarrod Maclean to destroy her. Not then. And not now.

She strode purposefully along the side of the gravel road, narrowing her eyes as the wind tossed up puffs of gritty dust. She hadn't even changed out of her faded jeans, well-worn cotton shirt and comfortable trainers. She could at least have tied back her hair, she reflected, knowing how windswept she was going to look when she arrived.

Aunt Isabel, who was always immaculately dressed, would frown her disapproval. Morgan was right—it was almost impossible to imagine that their mother and Aunt Isabel were sisters. Their home seemed to have always been filled with the sunny sound of their mother's laughter, while Isabel Maclean rarely so much as smiled.

And was Morgan right about Georgia? Had she become as withdrawn, as austere as their aunt? Surely not. Yet what had happened to her had to have left some mark on her. Anyone would have lost that certain *joie de vivre*.

Georgia's footsteps slowed. Perhaps it had really started with their mother's death seven years ago. It had been a terrible blow, for their father especially. He had taken her death badly, and for ages afterwards he had resorted to drink to carry him away from the grim reality of his loneliness. Georgia had truly feared his becoming an alcoholic. Maybe the worry of that had sent her more intensely into Jarrod's safe, strong arms.

For three years Georgia had watched her father drink his life away. Geoff Grayson had been drunk on that fateful night four years ago, but Georgia's plight had suddenly sobered him and he hadn't, to her knowledge, touched a drop since.

The huge old Maclean house came into view and Georgia's footsteps faltered again. It was a genuine colonial, the biggest of its type she had seen, extra rooms having been added twice since it was built in the late 1800s. But the additions had been expertly done and not a cent had been spared by Peter Maclean in keeping the house in good repair. It was quite a showpiece, for all that it was out in what was referred to as 'the sticks'.

Setting a firm resolve to be cool and composed, like Aunt Isabel, Georgia moved forward. And, anyway, as Lockie said, Jarrod would most probably be at his father's office in Ipswich. He was nothing if not conscientious, she mused bitterly. At least, he had been in the past.

'And what if Lockie should damage the car?' Isabel Maclean asked haughtily.

'Then we'll have it repaired.' Jarrod's expression was bland.

Georgia had explained Lockie's arrangement about the car to Aunt Isabel and she had insisted on fetching Jarrod, who had not been at the office but sitting with his father.

'Georgia—' he turned now from his stepmother 'are you in a hurry?'

'Well, Lockie will be wanting to go up to see about his tyre,' she said, her heart thumping with exasperating exhilaration at his nearness, his familiarity, the way he said her name.

'The sooner they get the tyre repaired, the sooner they'll bring the car back,' Isabel put in. 'Don't hold Georgia up, Jarrod.'

'Ten minutes,' he asked, barely acknowledging his stepmother's abrupt remonstrance.

Georgia hesitated, caught by the momentarily unguarded expression on her aunt's face. There was the usual irritated dissatisfaction and disapproval, and yet there was something else—something Georgia couldn't quite identify.

'Peter...' Jarrod paused. 'My father seems a little more comfortable this morning. Would you like to come in for a few minutes? He'd be pleased to see you.'

'I don't think that would be a good idea, Jarrod.' Isabel stepped forward. 'Too much talking only tires your father.'

'I know that, Isabel.' Jarrod frowned. 'But we'll do the talking.'

'It's still tiring for him,' Isabel persisted.

'He enjoys seeing people and we won't stay with him long.' He looked at Georgia. 'Coming?'

'Just remember how ill your father is.' Isabel's stance was all tension. 'And, Jarrod—' her eyes met his coldly '—don't upset him in any way.'

Some silent message passed between the two of them and Jarrod's mouth tightened. He took Georgia's elbow, unaware of the pressure of his fingers as they bit into her skin. But once they were out of the room his hand fell away immediately, and they moved down the hall to his father's suite without a word.

Georgia resisted the urge to rub her bruised arm, the place where his fingers had touched her burning as her nerve-endings exploded into life. Her senses reeled traitorously, uncontrollably, clamouring to make contact again, to have those sensitive hands take hold of her, pull her to him, mould her to his strong length, flesh to flesh.

No! Never again. You fool, Georgia Grayson, she angrily berated herself. He doesn't want you. He told you so four years ago. Can't you get that message through to your silly romantic heart?

Peter Maclean's rooms were at the back of the house. Isabel had had the section fitted up when her husband had suffered his first major attack. He had a full-time nurse who had her own quarters and no expense had been spared to make the old man comfortable. His bed was surrounded by complicated equipment on which his life depended.

He was lying in the pristine white bed in the centre of the room and even in the short time since Georgia had visited him she could see that he had failed. He'd lost even more weight and his veins stood out through paper-thin skin on his wasted hands. His eyes fluttered heavily open as they quietly entered the room and his hand moved in greeting, only to drop back on the sheet.

'Georgia,' the old man whispered with a faint smile shadowing his blue lips.

'Hello, Uncle Peter.' Georgia came forward and took the frail hand in hers. 'Jarrod says you're feeling a little better today.'

'Be up tomorrow, I reckon,' he joked breathlessly. 'Have a mind to chase Nurse Neal around the bed.'

Georgia laughed softly. 'You've been promising her that for weeks.'

'Keeps her on her toes.' His fingers tightened slightly on hers. 'I'm not seeing…as much of you, though.'

'No. I'm sorry about that, but I thought…' Georgia paused contritely. 'I mean, now that Jarrod's home…'

'You decided to desert me?'

'Oh, no. I just…'

Peter smiled again. 'Jarrod's all right but you're prettier than he is.' His eyes went past Georgia to his son. 'Get Georgia a drink, Jarrod.'

'No, thanks, Uncle Peter,' Georgia refused quickly. 'I'm afraid I can't stay long.'

Peter's fingers tightened convulsively. 'I'd like to talk—' he drew a quivering, painful breath '—to talk to you.'

Jarrod stepped forward and Georgia shot a swift glance at him, wondering if perhaps his father should be allowed to rest alone. But the look of raw pain she saw in Jarrod's eyes took her aback. And on the heels of that pain she watched him hesitate in uncharacteristic indecision.

'Maybe you should rest now, Peter,' he suggested softly.

'Rest later.' Peter moved his head irritably. 'Get Georgia...drink,' he finished on a rasp.

Jarrod paused again before he nodded and turned to Georgia. 'Tea?'

'Yes. Thank you.' She tried to marshal her jumbled thoughts.

What was going on here? She had a strongly intuitive feeling there was something more lurking beneath the even surface that Jarrod was trying to maintain. Suddenly it was almost as though he was loath to leave her alone with his father.

After Jarrod left the room it was a few minutes before Peter Maclean spoke.

'I want to talk...about Jarrod. I feel...' He sighed breathily. 'Once thought you and my son would... Never asked you before... What really happened, Georgia?'

Peter's chest rose and fell rapidly after the exertion of speaking and Georgia's first flash of the so-familiar pain that his question had brought was quickly overshadowed by her alarm.

'Don't talk, Uncle Peter,' she began, but his grip on her hand increased with surprising strength.

'Not dying yet, Georgia. But you...should humour me...in case I do.' He drew gasping breaths and then half smiled crookedly.

'Oh, Uncle Peter.' Georgia patted the hand that held hers. 'You mustn't overdo it.'

'Don't sidetrack. What happened...with my son?' he repeated.

Georgia shrugged with as much nonchalance as she could muster, fighting the rise of hurt that the mere thought of that time still caused her. Could she ever forget?

But what to tell his father? The truth? That his beloved son had been happy to take the childlike devotion she had so innocently given him, that he'd accepted that adoration but hadn't wanted to be tied down to marriage? Why marry a gauche teenager when other, more experienced women were available to warm his bed?

Like his own stepmother.

At the time Jarrod had denied the evidence which Georgia had considered to be overwhelming, but Aunt Isabel hadn't. She'd merely smiled at Georgia's stricken query, and now the remembered pain rose again to taunt her. All the while she'd loved him, worshipped him, and he'd used her, body and soul.

Your precious son broke my heart, Peter Maclean! she wanted to scream at him. And if you knew the truth it would break yours too.

But he was a frail, very sick old man.

'I guess it just didn't work out,' she said flatly, each word dragging painfully over her constricted throat muscles.

Peter's eyes seemed all of a sudden to pierce into her reserve, to cut down into the very essence of her being.

'That's what Jarrod said. Why?'

'We—well, we decided we didn't feel…didn't love each other enough to make a commitment,' Georgia mumbled lamely, not looking at Jarrod's father.

'A mutual decision?'

'Of course.' Georgia swallowed on the lie.

The old man was silent for some time, his breathing laboured. 'Don't suppose…you've changed your mind?'

Georgia shook her head, her heart aching painfully.

'Jarrod has.'

Her head shot up at his softly strained words.

CHAPTER SEVEN

'WHAT do you mean?' Georgia had almost as much trouble finding her voice as Peter had.

'I think my son...still loves you.'

'You're mistaken, Uncle Peter. I'm sorry, but—' She stopped as her mouth dried in agitation.

'And you? Do you...still love...him?'

'No!' she replied clearly, and the old man watched her with tired eyes.

'I don't...believe you,' he whispered.

Georgia could only stare back at him, no words coming.

'Someone has to...make...the first move. Forget silly pride. Pride's a...lonely...bedfellow. I can testify...to that.'

He closed his eyes and his grip on her hand slackened. Georgia stiffened in fright, but he exhaled a faint breath and she realised with relief that he was sleeping.

There was a sound behind her as Jarrod opened the door. He handed her a cup of tea as his eyes roved quickly, uneasily over her face.

'He's asleep,' she said softly, and Peter stirred, opening his eyes—eyes that were all at once clear and sharp. Gazing straight at Georgia.

'Jennifer? Darling Jenny.' A smile faintly lifted the corners of his mouth. 'Always were the prettiest girl I ever saw.'

He slipped into sleep again, more relaxed this time, and Georgia turned, perplexed, to Jarrod.

Jenny? That was her mother's name.

* * *

*   *   *

'I don't believe it.' Lockie entered the kitchen and turned a chair around, straddling it, his elbows resting on the back. 'Talk about bad luck.'

Georgia finished stacking the folded laundry into the basket. She was pondering over Peter Maclean's mistaking her for her mother. It was an understandable error, she could appreciate, for she knew she was very like her mother. Her father said the only difference was in the colour of her eyes. Jenny Grayson had had green eyes while Georgia's were brown, like her paternal grandmother's, her father maintained.

'Darling Jenny.' Had Uncle Peter really said that? And it wasn't so much what he'd said but the way he'd said it. 'Darling Jenny.' Had her mother been involved with Peter Maclean before she'd married their father? No. Georgia would never believe that. Her mother had loved their father so much.

Georgia hadn't been able to meet Jarrod's eyes when he'd returned with her tea. Jarrod still loves you, his father had said. Did he? And did she really care?

They'd left Uncle Peter, she and Jarrod, when they were sure he was fully asleep and, once out in the hall, Jarrod had hurried her out to the car as though he couldn't wait to be rid of her. Well, that was fine by her, she'd thought as she'd said a quick farewell to her aunt.

'Lockie will have the car back as soon as he can,' she had added stiffly as Jarrod opened the door for her.

'There's no hurry. I've got the wagon.' He'd closed the door and Georgia had switched on the ignition. 'And Georgia—' his hands had rested on the window-frame, preventing her from driving off '—Peter drifts off like that all the time, sort of slips into semi-consciousness, and he often gets confused. So don't take any notice of what he says.'

Georgia had looked up at him, into his eyes, and his lashes had fallen, masking his expression. Why had she got the impression quite suddenly that he had wanted to say more? His fingers had been white where he'd gripped the window-frame and there'd been a watchful tension in him.

'They all grew up around here,' she had said to him. 'My mother, Aunt Isabel and your father, so—' she shrugged '—I guess your father would have known my mother since she was born.'

Jarrod had nodded grimly and without a word he'd stepped back to allow her to drive away.

'Life's never dull, I'll say that!' Lockie was exclaiming now.

'What's wrong now?' Georgia forced herself to concentrate on what her brother was saying.

'Andy rang while you were out. Some of the other tenants where Andy has his new flat have complained about his practising again. And he's barely been there a week.' He threw his arms up. 'Can you believe it? They can't do that, can they? Throw him out, I mean?'

'Depends when he's been playing his drums,' Georgia replied, feeling some sympathy for Andy's fellow tenants.

'During the day, mostly.' Lockie frowned and shook his head. 'The landlord gave him a week to find somewhere else.'

'That's not long.'

'No. Pretty near impossible. So I told him he could move in here in the meantime.'

'You what?' Georgia stared at her brother.

'I said he could stay with us,' Lockie repeated blandly. 'What else could I do? Andy was in a spot. What are friends for?'

'But, Lockie, we don't have room,' Georgia told him.

'Andy can share with me. He doesn't mind.'

Georgia sighed exasperatedly. 'And what about all Andy's furniture and things?'

'We can store them under the house in the junk room. Dad's been onto me to sort through all that stuff, so I'll do it now and make space for Andy's gear. In fact I've already made a start on it, while you were collecting the car. It's only for a few weeks till Andy finds somewhere else. We can practise here too, during the day. We haven't got any neighbours to disturb.'

Lockie was right about that. Their nearest neighbour was Uncle Peter and there were acres of bushland between their houses.

'You don't really mind, do you, Georgia?' Lockie asked. 'Andy'll pay his way; he's not a bludger.'

Georgia shook her head. 'I guess, if you're prepared to share your room with him, what can I say? When's he moving in?'

Lockie grinned and crossed to give her a squeeze. 'Thanks, Georgia. We'll move most of his stuff in the morning but Evan's coming over to pick up the van as soon as I get the tyre fixed. He's going to collect some of Andy's stuff while I finish clearing the way downstairs in the storeroom. We've got it all worked out.'

'So it would seem,' remarked Georgia drily. 'Dad will think we've turned the place into a motel or something.'

'I'll ring Dad later, before we leave for the club. Now, I'd best be off to get the tyre. See you later.'

After lunch Georgia determinedly began poring over her studies again. The boys were downstairs, sorting out and storing Andy's gear. At one stage she had heard the faint strumming of a guitar but all was quiet now and she glanced at the time. Setting aside her books, she went into the kitchen to boil the kettle. What she needed was a nice cup of tea.

'Georgia?' Lockie's footsteps clattered up the back steps. He burst into the kitchen with Andy, Evan and Ken on his heels, and the kitchen's usually ample proportions became decidedly wanting.

'I'm making a cup of tea. Anyone want a cup?' Georgia asked.

'Later, sis,' Lockie said, seeming a little preoccupied. 'Georgia, I can't believe this. Do you remember it?' He held up a creased and dog-eared music book.

'My old songbook? I thought it had been thrown out years ago. Where did you find it?'

'In the junk room, with a stack of sheet music.' Lockie
flipped the pages. 'Georgia, these songs—where did you get
them? You've written them out by hand. Do you remember
where you copied them from?'

Georgia took the book from him and laughed embarrassedly. 'They're not professional songs, just some silly tunes I
wrote when I fancied being a songwriter.'

'You wrote them?' Ken gasped.

'Silly tunes? Are you nuts, Georgia?' Andy exclaimed at
the same time. 'They're fantastic, girl. We want to use them
in the act.'

Georgia's eyes went from Andy's bearded face to her
brother. 'You can't be serious. I was just fiddling around with
them. They're amateurish.'

'Would that some pros could be that amateurish.' Ken grimaced. 'I wish I'd written them.'

'We want to copyright them, Georgia, and add them to our
routine.' Lockie took the book back from Georgia's nerveless
fingers and opened it at the first page.

The kettle whistled and Georgia absently switched it off.
'Lockie, I don't think—' she began, but Lockie held up his
hand.

'Just hang on, Georgia. Give us a few chords on the guitar,
Ken.'

Ken Wilson put one foot on a chair and settled Lockie's old
folk guitar across his knee. Evan and Lockie stood behind him
so they could read the music over his shoulder and they began
to sing, softly harmonising with Lockie's lead.

Georgia listened self-consciously and then there was a moment's silence when they'd finished.

'That's no silly tune,' Andy said seriously.

'I guess it sounded all right,' Georgia agreed uneasily,
somewhat amazed at Lockie's rendition of a song she scarcely
recalled putting on paper. Her songwriting phase had been
short-lived, existing only until pain had taken precedence.
Georgia's lips tightened. Pain caused by Jarrod Maclean.

'All right?' Lockie appealed. 'Bit of an understatement, wouldn't you say, Georgia?' He turned the page. 'We quickened this one up.'

Ken strummed an up-tempo beat. 'Come and sing along, Georgia.'

She joined them, humming and then taking up the lyrics.

'There are eight songs here, all great,' Lockie enthused when they'd finished the song. He flipped the pages over to the back. 'But this one's the best. The greatest.'

The loose sheet slipped out and Lockie laid it on the table.

The title, printed in her own neat hand, hit Georgia a paralysing blow. She felt the colour drain from her face and just as quickly return to wash her cheeks in a fiery blush.

'No!' she got out. 'Not that one, Lockie. That's private.' She made to snatch up the page, intent on crumpling it, but Lockie swept it out of her reach. 'Lockie, please! Throw it away. I didn't mean to leave it there. It wasn't...I don't want...I should have burned it.' Her voice shook agitatedly.

'Over my dead body!' Ken exclaimed.

'And mine,' agreed Andy.

'I'd kill to have written that beauty, Georgia,' Ken told her seriously. 'And no one destroys it while I'm around.'

'It's not that good,' she entreated. 'I never even worked on it.'

'It doesn't need it. And you're right about one thing, Georgia,' Lockie said. 'It's not good. It's just bloody sensational.'

Georgia flushed again. 'I couldn't... I can't...' She drew a shaky breath. 'What I mean is, I never meant for anyone to hear it.'

Ken gave a chuckle. 'I can sort of understand that. It's a pretty sexy song for an innocent like you.'

Georgia's face grew redder and the boys laughed.

'Going to tell us where you picked up the experience to write that song, Georgia?' teased Evan.

'Marvellous what a bit of imagination will uncover—hey, Georgia?' Ken winked.

'OK, guys.' Lockie broke in, and the other three laughed louder.

'Brother to the rescue.' Andy slapped Lockie on the back, not noticing the way Lockie's eyes slid embarrassedly from his sister's.

'We were just kidding you, Georgia,' said Andy good-naturedly. 'But that song will be a hit, make no joke about that. We all think so.'

'A hit? Wh-what do you mean?' Georgia stammered as she fought her pressing memories with all the self-control she could assemble. 'Lockie?'

'What Andy means is we've all decided—'

'Unanimously, so to speak,' interrupted Andy.

'We've all decided,' Lockie continued, 'it's the song we've been looking for to record. We've wanted a song that was strong enough to be the feature of our album. This is it, Georgia.'

'But I told you it was private, Lockie. I don't want it performed. It's—well, it's… I'd be too embarrassed,' Georgia finished lamely.

'Come on, Georgia, just bear with us. Don't you want to be a wealthy songwriter?' Lockie grinned appealingly.

'But, Lockie—' she began, and Andy gave another chuckle.

'It's one of the sexiest songs I've ever heard and we've decided you can sing it tonight, Georgia, to test it out. We reckon it'll be fantastic.'

'Me sing it tonight?' she squeaked. 'No way! You guys know I'm only helping you out until Mandy gets back next week. Two nights only. That doesn't mean I want to learn new material.'

Lockie shot the others a warning look and faced his sister. 'You already know the song, Georgia, and we can practise it now,' he said softly, and Georgia stared at him speechlessly.

'You have to be kidding. And any new material can wait till Mandy gets back,' Georgia told him firmly.

'Georgia—' Andy began, but Lockie stopped him with a negating move of his hand.

'We've been told D.J. Delaney will definitely be at the club tonight. This song will really grab him. It'll make us, sis.'

Georgia rubbed her temple.

'We need you, Georgia, and we need your song to attract D.J. Delaney's attention. That song—' he indicated the sheet on the table '—will be a number-one best-seller, and with the rest of your material on the album it will sell like hot cakes. I tell you, we're onto a winner here.'

'He's right, Georgia,' Andy agreed, and the other two nodded.

'Oh, for heaven's sake!' Georgia shook her head. 'If you do by some miracle get to make this record all I can see is a faint chance for you. How many locally produced records really make it? I'll bet the statistics are phenomenal for those that don't.' Georgia pushed aside the thought that she was voicing Jarrod's arguments of last night. 'And I can't see that this would be any different. You'd need diabolical luck.'

'Have you lost your ears, girl?' Lockie exclaimed. 'Can't you hear how fantastic it sounds? That one song on its own will take the public by storm.' He pursed his lips. 'Look, we're not asking you to make the record, Georgia. Mandy will be back by then. But we need you for the show tonight.'

'You're not just any female voice, you know.' Andy grinned at her. 'You're top class, like Mandy. How about just running through it with us, to see how it sounds?'

Georgia glanced from one to the other and sighed. 'All right. But I think you're exaggerating about the song.'

Ken strummed a chord and Georgia began to sing. In no time the boys were harmonising and the pure sounds of the melody filled the kitchen. And Georgia didn't even have to read the lyrics. She found she remembered each and every one of them. With the boys watching her she managed to remain detached, while one small part of her mourned for that so-in-love young girl she had been when she'd written the song.

'What did I tell you, sis?' Lockie exclaimed when they'd spent an hour or so going over the tune. 'It's dynamite. Mandy will love it.'

'I still don't want to sing it, Lockie,' Georgia said, and the boys groaned.

'You have to, Georgia,' Andy appealed. 'We're desperate to make the most of this break.'

'It all hinges on you, sis.' Her brother brushed his fair hair off his forehead.

'But I don't want that responsibility, Lockie.'

'Georgia—'

'I can't take this any more.' Georgia swung away from them. 'I'm going for a walk. I need some space and time to think.'

Scarcely knowing what she intended, Georgia went down the back stairs, her footsteps taking her across to the back fence. She forced open the gate, which was stiff on its hinges, closed it after her and took the pathway through the scrub.

With a part-anticipatory, part-antipathetic feeling of *déjà vu* she walked along the well-remembered track, only stopping when she came to the creek, or rather creek bed. After rain it could run, churning the sandy bottom, but more often than not it was just a string of shallow potholes.

The old bridge had gone and a sturdy footbridge had replaced the splintering timbers. Her father and Uncle Peter had seen to that. Afterwards, Georgia stood gazing at the bridge and choked off a slightly hysterical laugh. A classic case of shutting the stable door after the horse had bolted.

In agitation she turned away to raise her eyes to the grassy bank. To their special place.

Her lips twisted cynically but she found herself moving forward, scrambling up the bank to stand beneath the leafy overhang. She gazed at the view—the creek, the dry, grassy paddocks, the gums and she-oaks and wattles, the few cattle grazing in the distance. And the track that continued on to the Macleans'. To Jarrod.

Oh, Jarrod. Her pain escaped on a quivering sigh.

Slowly she sank down to sit on the sparse grass that in the present dry spell valiantly tried to cover the sandy soil.

A cold ache began in the pit of her stomach and she drew up her knees, clasping her arms around them.

She hadn't been here for years. Hadn't wanted to revisit the place that held such painful memories. Yet at first she'd haunted the place so hopefully, so sure he'd come back.

But, of course, he hadn't, and eventually she'd made herself brutally face the fact. Like in the lyrics of the classic old song, he'd done her wrong. And he wasn't coming back to make it right.

But she still couldn't understand why he'd done what he had. After all they'd shared. Especially the night she'd written that song.

She had to admit that, with the boys harmonising, her ballads took better shape than she could have imagined when she'd written them, over four years ago.

But that other song—she didn't think she could bring herself to sing that special song in public. Special song? She lashed out at herself with bitterness. It had only been special then because at the time she had been floating in a state of guileless delusion.

When she'd written it the words had burst forth with little conscious thought on her part. The lyrics had been an extension of the wondrously ecstatic aftermath of Jarrod's lovemaking. Of his hands on her body. And his lips. Georgia tried to block it out of her mind.

Back then she had been so youthfully sure that her music would make her into a household name. Celebrated songwriter, Georgia Grayson.

She pulled a face. When she'd written that special song she had changed her aspirations in one minor detail. Celebrated songwriter, Georgia Maclean.

She gave a softly bitter laugh that caught throatily somewhere in her chest. And she'd been convinced of for ever. For
ever. Georgia sighed.

What a mess she'd made of everything back then. And what
a fantastic job she'd made of putting the past behind her. If
she had been successful she would have been able to sing that
song without a qualm. It was a song just like any other song.
Words and music.

She was such a wimp. If she had any gumption at all she'd
force herself to sing it, and then perhaps she could finally
exorcise the ghosts.

Georgia got resolutely to her feet. Languishing here like a
wronged Victorian maiden in a decline was cowardly and
spineless. And that was what she'd been since Jarrod came
home.

She'd allowed his reappearance to get to her, let it feed her
insecurities. But the time had come for her to stand up and
face it. Otherwise she'd come to hate herself.

She slithered down the bank and began following the path
towards home.

And this farce of pretending to Jarrod that she was Country
Blues' regular singer just to get under his skin was ridiculous.
Why was she doing it? For revenge? Nothing she could do or
say could make Jarrod suffer enough for what had happened.
The perpetrators never did suffer. Only their victims bore the
scars. Now she had to live with them, get on with her life as
she had been doing before he'd come home.

And what was one more performance anyway? Mandy
would be back in time for the following weekend's stint and
could be part of Lockie's recording dreams. And her brother
was right—he, all of them, needed this chance.

She rounded the corner of the track just as Lockie was
climbing the gate, and behind him stood Andy and a tall,
broad-shouldered, so familiar, dark-haired man.

'There you are, Georgia,' Lockie said quickly. 'We were
getting worried. We didn't know where you'd gone—'

'And it was time for dinner,' Georgia finished for him, her voice just a little thin and breathy.

'Ken and Evan have gone home to eat and change and we've invited Jarrod to sample your cooking,' Andy told her affably.

'As a thanks for letting me borrow his car,' Lockie explained hastily.

'Oh.' Georgia's heart had sunk, her new-found control wavering, but she straightened her backbone and lifted her chin. 'Deciding to live dangerously, Jarrod?' she quipped quite evenly.

He raised a dark brow. 'There's always the take-away joint to fall back on.'

'Let their tastebuds be their guides.' Lockie put his arm around his sister and then turned and gave the lopsided gate a kick. 'Damn thing's stuck again. That's another job to do. We'll have to climb over it, I guess.' With the ease of long-legged agility he vaulted the fence.

Georgia tried the gate but it wouldn't budge. 'Do you mean I have to scramble over it too? I'll probably break my neck.'

Andy sprang across and picked her up in his arms, holding her high. 'What you need, fair damsel, is a strong knight in shining armour to ride to your rescue in your time of need.' He beamed. 'Sir Andrew of the Drums at your service.' As though she were a featherweight he deposited her on the other side of the fence. 'I've been telling you for years just to call and I'll come at the double.'

With a laugh Georgia turned to thank him, but her eyes were drawn to Jarrod, surprising the burning light of plain, old-fashioned jealousy in the look he was giving the unsuspecting drummer. Andy was totally oblivious of the tension in the air, keeping his arm around her as they walked back to the house.

'Did you notice how strong I am, Georgia?' he teased her, and she made a show of feeling the bulging muscles in his upper arm.

'How could I miss it? No wonder you're so good at moving

furniture. And I thought you were just a pretty face.' She knew
a surge of heady power as she followed Jarrod, his body taut
with silent tension.

Their early-evening meal passed off quite well, although
Georgia couldn't later remember what they had talked about.
Lockie opened some wine and they laughed a lot. At least, the
men did. Georgia remained somewhat apart from them, and
after the meal when they went out onto the veranda she cried
off from joining them, deciding to wash her hair.

She took her time in the bathroom, blow-drying her hair,
leaving it flowing in soft tendrils about her face. She donned
a fresh pair of jeans and a loose cotton shirt. Now, she supposed, she should make some coffee.

She walked into the hallway and straight into Lockie. He
was returning from the kitchen with two cold cans of beer.

'I guess you don't want coffee,' she said, indicating the
beer, and Lockie shook his head.

'Georgia, about tonight at the club. And the song.'

'You don't give up, do you, Lockie?'

'Will you do it?' he persisted.

Georgia sighed loudly. 'We've barely had a run-through.'

'The boys and I practised while you were walking. We're
ready. And you were fine before. Anyway, we can do a quick
rehearsal when we get to the club.'

'Lockie, I can't.'

He sighed. 'OK, sis. If it brings back too many unhappy
memories.' Lockie lowered his voice. 'Did you write it for
Jarrod?'

'Don't be ridiculous!' Georgia bit out.

'Well…' He shrugged. 'I thought, as you were being so
determined about not singing it, you must have written it for
him and that you must still be hurt over—well, over everything that happened.'

Georgia stiffened. 'I'm not. And your imagination's working overtime.'

'Why else would you be so adamant?'

'Oh, for heaven's sake. I'll sing it. It's just a song.'

Lockie smiled crookedly. 'You will? That's great, Georgia. You've probably just saved our careers.'

'Humph!'

'Coming outside?' he asked. 'Andy's gone to have a shower so there's only Jarrod and me.'

Georgia hesitated. 'I should be getting ready for tonight…' she began, and Lockie frowned.

'Georgia,' he appealed. 'There's plenty of time and you're making it pretty damn obvious.'

'What are you talking about?'

'You know very well what I mean.' He was grim-faced. 'You're still giving Jarrod the cold shoulder, aren't you?'

'Don't start that again, Lockie. I really do need to iron my clothes for tonight.'

Lockie glared at her and then, shaking his head, he continued out onto the veranda.

Georgia lingered in the hallway before returning to the kitchen, putting away crockery, wiping down already clean counter-tops. She ironed her outfit and eventually made her way to the front of the house, listening for sounds of male voices coming from the veranda, but she could hear none and she relaxed. Jarrod must have gone home.

Unsuspectingly she walked out onto the veranda only to stop short at the sight of Lockie and Jarrod sitting back in easy chairs, their feet resting on the low veranda railings. Both men turned to face her.

Jarrod's glance was as impassive as ever. 'You look nice and cool, Georgia.'

She could hardly re-enter the house, so with much reluctance she strolled forward. 'It's going to be another hot evening, isn't it?' she said as she gazed out into the gathering dusk, watching a flock of birds fly over, black specks in the twilight sky.

'It'll be hot on stage at the club if they haven't adjusted the air-conditioning.' Lockie took a gulp of his beer. 'I thought I'd melt last night.'

'Would you like another drink?' Georgia asked, and both men declined.

'I think I might try phoning Mandy just on the off chance she's returned early.' Lockie stood up. 'I'll bring us some coffee when I come back.' And once again he left her alone with Jarrod.

CHAPTER EIGHT

GEORGIA could feel her muscles tense, her nerve-endings quiver, and she couldn't stop her gaze from finding his. He was watching her and their eyes met. Meshed.

And the fire burned. Georgia felt the warmth grow inside her, spreading so quickly that her breath caught somewhere in her chest. Did he feel it? Was it eating away at him too? Did his body cry out for her until the pain was a deep, yearning ache inside him?

She turned away to lean on the veranda rail in case he read the wanting in her eyes. Perhaps she should let him see, her inner voice suggested. Remind him of their past love. But she wasn't in love with him any more, she cried back.

Love! She felt her lips twist bitterly. Love hurt, and hurt killed love, didn't it? And she had no desire to suffer that way again.

So, if she wasn't in love with him, then this turmoil inside must be purely physical. Her body hadn't forgotten him—that was the whole trouble.

Lust! It was pure, unadulterated lust. Perhaps she *should* let him see, make him aware that she was available for the sins of the flesh. And maybe then she could get him out of her system completely. But leave love four years behind her where it belonged.

'Lockie was telling me that the owner of the club has arranged for a well-known record producer to come along to see your performance tonight,' Jarrod said into the silence, and Georgia shrugged.

'Lockie seems to have high hopes.'

'But not you, obviously. So you have no aspirations to become the next Anne Murray or Reba McEntire?'

'Hardly!' Georgia gave a short laugh. 'As you said, it wouldn't fit in with my career.'

'You really would prefer that to the spotlights?' he asked.

Georgia shrugged again. 'As you said, it's more secure. I may even get to own my own bookshop one day.'

'You never struck me as being a career woman.'

But you never really knew me, she longed to say, or you'd never have hurt me so deeply.

'Not a note of chauvinism, Jarrod?' she made herself tease lightly. 'Why shouldn't I want to make the book trade a lifetime career? I thought that was what you were advocating last week?'

'I just remember you as having more romantic leanings—say, a poet or a songwriter.'

Wife and mother, she burned to throw back at him. Wasn't that being a romantic fool? Say it, Georgia, she goaded herself. Say it! And see how the cool, reserved Jarrod Maclean reacts.

He'd turned to glance sideways at her, perhaps sensing her vibes, but before he could continue she spoke.

'Poet, songwriter, wife and mother?' She actually heard the words spill from her mouth.

Some fleeting expression, one she couldn't quite pinpoint, passed over his face before he had himself under control once more.

Was he not as composed, as self-possessed as he'd like her to believe?

'Always the romantic, wasn't I, Jarrod?' Georgia was amazed at the calm, even timbre of her voice, while inside old love battled renewed hate, anger attacked despair, and her rekindled attraction mutinously fought her well-stoked self-disgust.

Almost imperceptibly Jarrod flinched, as though she'd

struck him, and his face paled, his eyes bleak, all at once naked with a deep agony.

She'd reached him, Georgia recognised, and part of her rejoiced. Well, the voice inside her said matter-of-factly, she'd taken aim just as she'd been wanting to ever since his return, and it seemed she'd scored a direct hit because it appeared as though her barb had gone home. And if she evoked a reaction he must at some stage have cared, perhaps was feeling some regret.

Hope flared but she quickly quelled it with practised ease. She was a bigger fool now than she'd ever been before. If he'd loved her he'd never have done what he had.

Then why was she again feeling guilt for causing him pain? He was the wrongdoer. She hadn't broken *his* heart and left him to pick up the pieces. Nor had she expected him to shake hands now and chat as friends, pretending it had never happened, as though they had never known each other so intimately.

So why the pain, Georgia?

'Actually, I thought you might have married,' he was saying in a flat, even tone. 'I half expected you to be settled down with a couple of kids.'

Something stirred deep inside her, a fragmented memory of that time of struggle for life, and she swung slightly away from him so he was unable to see her face, read the sorrow she knew was written so plainly there.

'Did you? Why?' She had herself under control again and turned back to him.

Jarrod shrugged. 'I don't know. You're an attractive girl. The guys around town couldn't help but notice.' He paused. 'Is there anyone special?'

'Perhaps,' Georgia exaggerated. 'One or two.' What a joke! She hadn't so much as looked at another man since he'd left.

'Andy?' He twisted the empty can in his fingers.

'Andy's a good friend,' was all she said.

'So you're not in love with him?' he asked, his eyes narrowed on something in the darkness beyond the lit veranda.

How could he even say the word? He couldn't begin to know what those four letters meant.

'Love?' Georgia pulled a posed grimace. 'I really don't think love…' she paused disparagingly '…has anything to do with it.'

His jaw had tensed and a tiny pulse beat near his mouth but he didn't look at her.

She hadn't exactly lied to him. She wasn't in love with anyone, but her intonation had been such that Jarrod could have been forgiven for reading lust for love. Yet now, perversely, she was angry lest he judge her. But something drove her.

'Perhaps I prefer playing the field.'

He did turn then, and she met his gaze defiantly.

Jarrod shook his head. 'I don't think so, Georgia,' he said quietly as he stood up and moved over to lean on the veranda railing, just feet from her. And far too close.

Her laugh was brittle, a little high. 'Why not? I grew up, Jarrod. I'm not a green teenager any more.'

'No, I suppose you're not,' he agreed.

'And perhaps I've decided I can have it all. A career. Relationships.'

'Relationships? Plural?' The shadow of emotion in his voice had every nerve in her body on full alert.

Her eyes flew to meet his in time to see his own gaze move slowly downwards over her full breasts, and her skin burned beneath her suddenly transparent shirt. As though he'd touched her. The way he used to do.

There was a more tangible tension in him now and Georgia held her breath, waiting, wanting. Then he had relaxed and the moment passed. And Georgia knew the familiar ache of loss, and she despised herself.

'Actually, you're right, Jarrod.' She folded her arms over

her breasts, aware of their still aroused state, knowing it would be visible through the thin cotton covering them.

'Quite frankly,' she continued, 'I don't feel I need a man—any man. I tried it once and, believe me, I didn't much care for it.'

'Georgia…'

She didn't need to hear the strangled sound in his voice to know that another barb had found its mark. And she suddenly realised, in her effort to avenge herself on him, just how transparent she was being. She was all but laying her wounded soul bare before him. Where was her pride?

She tried for a light laugh, and almost succeeded. 'Love, no. Sex? Now that's a different matter. I guess the best lesson I learned was not to combine the two. It only complicates everything, don't you think?'

'What do you want me to say to that, Georgia?' he asked flatly, not looking at her.

'Why, nothing, Jarrod.' Georgia shrugged, tired of the conversation now herself but somehow unable to end it. 'But what's good enough for a man is good enough for a woman. Don't you think that's fair? Modern science has made it just as easy for a woman to sow her wild oats as it's been for a man. And practice makes perfect, you must agree.'

He stepped towards her, taking hold of her, his fingers biting into her arms, drawing her savagely against the hardness of his body. She could feel the tautness rampant in every inch of him and her own senses responded with sickening spontaneity.

His dark head lowered towards her, his mouth fastening onto hers, his kiss a cruel parody of the caresses they had once shared. Her lips were crushed beneath his, his tongue plundering. And Georgia found her traitorous body responding. She pressed herself against his hardness, moulding her curves to the strong, hard length of him.

It had been too long; she tried to exonerate her behaviour—behaviour that one tiny, still rational part of her vehemently decried. She had been waiting for this moment for four long years, this sybaritic part of her lying dormant, waiting to be woken.

And Jarrod, too, was totally aroused by their kiss. Georgia felt the heady hardness of him straining against her as his hands held her locked to him, fingers splayed out over her buttocks.

After no time or all time their lips separated and they drew gulping breaths. Georgia's heartbeats raced inside her chest, the thunder of them echoing in her ears. Her darkened eyes rose, devoured his full mouth, met his stormy gaze. She licked her suddenly dry lips and she felt the muscles in his thighs tense.

They stood like that, neither moving, until Jarrod drew a deep, shuddering breath, his face gauntly pale. With a super-human effort he controlled himself, his punishing grip suddenly relaxing. Then he had released her.

'I'm sorry,' he said thickly. 'I didn't mean to do that, to hurt you.'

Georgia rubbed her bruised arms. But she was finding that her physical pain was fading much faster than the other, more potent feelings he had aroused.

'I guess I'm on something of a short fuse these days, what with Peter...' He took another breath and sat down again, his movements measured, almost mechanical, as though he was deliberately forcing himself to relax. 'But I shouldn't have done that. Kissed you.'

'No. You—' Georgia cleared her throat and turned away from him. 'We shouldn't.'

There was a moment's thick silence. 'Growing up together the way we did, I suppose I still see myself as a big brother, if you like, wanting to look after you.'

'That wasn't a big-brother kiss,' Georgia said huskily.

'I'm sorry, Georgia. You don't have to worry. It won't happen again.'

What if she told him she wanted it to happen again, and go on happening again, and again? Georgia swallowed, hot colour washing her face, and she was glad she'd turned away from him.

'No. It won't,' she said with as much conviction as she could muster.

'Then maybe we should just forget it happened and change the subject,' he said, and she knew he was running his hand through his thick hair.

The nerves in the pit of her stomach lurched again and she bit her lip.

'Lockie tells me he has some fantastic new material by an unknown songwriter,' he continued, as though nothing had happened, and Georgia turned to blink at him incredulously.

'He means some old stuff I wrote ages ago,' she made herself reply. 'He thinks they might be suitable for his album.'

'*You* wrote?' It was his turn to gaze across at her and she could see that he was recalling their previous conversation.

Poet. Songwriter. Wife. Mother. And lover. The words spun crazily in Georgia's head. They were almost like the lyrics of a song itself.

'I remember you used to write some pretty good ones. And will you be recording these songs with Lockie's band?' he asked flatly.

'I think Lockie's thoughts of recording contracts are a little premature.'

'Not by the sound of it. But I thought you weren't inclined to make singing your career?' Jarrod picked up his can of beer in its insulated casing and took an almost casual sip.

Georgia shrugged. 'I'm not.'

'Well, if you don't intend to make the record with Lockie I think you should tell him so,' Jarrod remarked, when Georgia thought the silence stretching between them would deafen them both.

'I have told Lockie I'm not recording with him. I'd hardly have time to fit in recording sessions with my job at the bookshop.'

'I thought he said—' Jarrod stopped and frowned. 'Are you

sure Lockie isn't getting carried away and expecting you to go along with him? I mean, I can set him straight if you want me to.'

Georgia raised her eyebrows. 'Why would I need you to do that?'

Jarrod shrugged. 'Lockie seems to have the knack of running roughshod over you all, exerting his charm all the way, of course.' He smiled faintly.

'I can stand up for myself, Jarrod.' Georgia could feel her anger rise—anger that was out of all proportion to the crime. What gave him the right to the position of the great, almighty protector?

'I know you can,' he was agreeing. 'I just thought it might help to have some backup for a change. And, considering you get so nervous before going on stage, it hardly seems worth putting yourself through it night after night.' He looked up at her. 'I'd say you were pretty uptight when I drove you to the club last night. You always used to suffer from stage fright.'

Used to. Yesterday. That was then, Jarrod. She didn't want to talk about that now. Not with him. Never with him. She wanted to pour her pain over him, cut him the way reminders of the past sliced through her.

I'm surprised you remember, Jarrod.

Had she actually voiced those caustic words? Her eyes skimmed his face but obviously she hadn't, for his expression was one of apparently relaxed enquiry.

She took a steadying breath, tired now of the whole thing. 'Look, Jarrod, I'm not Country Blues' usual lead singer,' she said flatly. There, it was out. 'I'm only standing in for Mandy until she gets back from New Zealand. Mandy, Lockie's fiancée, sings with the band; she has been for the best part of a year.'

His gaze held hers for a long moment. 'Then why did you tell me you were?'

'I didn't tell you I was. You simply misunderstood Lockie.'

'That's splitting hairs, isn't it?' Anger gravelled his voice.

'It's no big deal, is it?' Georgia stated defensively. 'I just didn't think I was bound to tell you everything.'

His eyes fell. 'No,' he said quietly. 'No, I don't suppose you are.'

'I couldn't exactly leave Lockie in the lurch when he got this big break.'

'No.' Jarrod grimaced at his nearly empty can of beer. 'And you do have a great voice,' he said softly, without expression.

Georgia's gaze was drawn downwards. She was half standing, perched on the veranda rail, while he was seated, and of their own accord her eyes hungrily roamed the contours of his face. His dark lashes fanned over the tanned skin drawn over his cheekbones and she realised suddenly that he was thinner. His jeans didn't fit as snugly over his narrow hips, and his face looked tired and more than a little gaunt. Was he…?

No! He was worried and upset about Uncle Peter's precarious health. It would be a strain on anyone, knowing that your father's life was slowly ebbing away. He wasn't pining over a lost love the way she had done.

A thought she'd had before returned vividly to taunt her. Unless there was a girl in the States he'd had to leave behind. Why wouldn't he have had girls in the past four years? There'd probably been dozens.

An aching pain again stabbed in the region of Georgia's heart and she almost allowed a bitter laugh to escape at the idea that she was burningly jealous of every one of them.

'Lockie thinks the songs he's chosen for the album are great. He's positive one song will be a smash hit.' Jarrod broke in on her speculations. 'What's it called? Have I heard it?'

She stiffened, silently begging him not to ask her to talk about that song. She'd never played it for him.

'There're a couple of tunes the boys have been fiddling around with.' She turned away to gaze unseeingly into the night.

'Lockie sounded as though he thought one of the songs was pretty special.'

Georgia shrugged.

'He said it was the sexiest song he'd ever heard.'

Was there a note of censure in his voice? Georgia's lips tightened. She was being supersensitive. Overreacting. Trying to read into his words, his tone any small intimation that meant he might still care. The way Lockie said he did.

'Sexy songs seem to sell,' she remarked tritely, and he was silent for so long that she couldn't prevent herself from sliding a sideways glance at him.

He was once again contemplating the can of beer he held, and from his expression it could have contained sand rather than the cold amber liquid. Her throat tightened as her eyes lingered on him. How she'd love to reach out to him the way she used to do in her spontaneous innocence, cradle his head against her, smooth the fine lines that radiated from the corner of his clear blue eyes. Laughter lines. And yet he gave the impression he rarely so much as smiled any more.

He glanced up then and caught her looking at him, couldn't help but see the glow of remembered passion that she was too slow to hide.

For one minuscule fraction of a second she saw an answering flame burn just as feverishly in his eyes before his lashes fell to shutter it from her.

But it was enough to set Georgia's heartbeats racing in her chest, tripping erratically over themselves in their sudden agitation. No, the fire hadn't died in him any more than it had been extinguished inside her. That kiss had been an honest reaction on both their parts. Yet now she suspected he was taking great pains to prove to her that it had been otherwise.

Unless she was misinterpreting again. Maybe it had been no more than a blatant physical attraction between them. Then and now. And, perhaps because he recalled how hard she had taken it when she'd broken off their sordid little affair, he had no intention of becoming involved again, was taking no chances on a repeat performance.

Dear Lord! She had no inclination to go through that night

again either. That dreadful night was printed indelibly, ineradicably on her mind.

When she closed her eyes she could almost smell the distinctive heavy scent of the blossoming golden wattle, just about feel the sensation of the cool breeze in her hair as she'd run sure-footedly along the track in the fast-gathering dusk, clutching her fantastic secret inside her. She had scarcely been able to wait to see Jarrod, to tell him.

The lights had been on in the Maclean living room. She'd known Uncle Peter was away in Hong Kong, and as she'd approached the house she'd seen Aunt Isabel's immaculately groomed figure pause by the lighted window. Isabel's hand had fluttered to finger the brooch she wore on the collar of her tailored blouse.

Georgia had taken the steps two at a time, her sneakers almost soundless on the wooden treads. She'd lifted her hand to press the chimes beside the open door but had hesitated as she'd heard her aunt speak.

It wasn't that Georgia had intended to eavesdrop, it was simply that something in Isabel's tone had held her momentarily motionless.

'You know what you'll have to do, don't you, Jarrod?' Isabel said.

'I want to speak to my father first.' Jarrod's voice was almost unrecognisable, and Georgia drew in a sharp, surprised breath.

'What good will that do?' Isabel remarked in a barbed tone. 'It won't change anything.'

'How can you calmly stand there and tell me this? How could you live with it? With him?'

'Your father asked me to marry him and in those days we did what was expected of us. What else could I do? I was a spinster and didn't want to be a burden on anyone, especially my only sister. Some of us did the honourable thing, Jarrod.'

'You call any of it honourable? Honourable, my eye! What kind of man was he?'

Georgia heard Jarrod swear, using a word she'd never actually heard spoken, and she stepped anxiously towards the doorway.

'Why didn't he marry *her* in the first place? Wouldn't that have been doing your so honourable thing?' Jarrod asked hoarsely.

'She didn't love him.'

Jarrod swore again.

'You must realise what sort of man your father was.' Isabel's voice was a sneer. 'Your mother—'

'Leave my mother out of this,' Jarrod bit out with a quiet, potent anger that made Georgia hesitate again in the doorway.

Isabel gave an exclamation of disgust.

'Why didn't *he* tell me this, Isabel? Was he such a coward he had to opt out and leave it up to you to do his dirty work?'

'He didn't know. She didn't tell him.'

'She didn't…? For pity's sake, Isabel, why not?'

'Who knows—?'

'Why didn't you do something about it?' Jarrod broke in.

'It was scarcely my place to tell tales.'

'Tales!' Exasperation was heavy in his tone. 'Are you trying to tell me my father still doesn't know?'

'I didn't say that, Jarrod. Perhaps he suspects. Look, must we go over and over it all? I'm only sorry I have to be the one to tell you.' Her aunt's tone had dropped, holding more emotion than Georgia had ever heard in her voice before.

'I just bet you are!' Jarrod grated rawly.

'I simply thought you should know before—' her aunt paused '—before things went too far.'

'Too far?' Jarrod's voice broke on a hollow groan of such anguish that Georgia stepped into the hallway, but her aunt's surprisingly provocative tone made her pause again as she was about to enter the living room.

'Jarrod?' Isabel appealed in a low, silky purr—another tone Georgia had never before heard in her aunt's voice. 'Look, this is best sorted out now, isn't it? You can just tell her it's over, that you've changed your mind. Georgia's young. She'll find someone else quickly enough.'

Georgia's heartbeats accelerated in shock as the meaning of her aunt's words hit her like a thunderbolt. Jarrod had changed his mind about her? But he couldn't have. Could he?

'Someone else?' Jarrod repeated quietly.

'Yes, someone else. And so will you. Why, any number of young women would jump at the chance. You're attractive—' Isabel continued confidently, and Jarrod cut in with a desolate laugh.

'And this someone else I'm going to find…' he jeered. 'No doubt you'll be putting yourself at the head of the line. Well, Isabel? Won't you? You always have. Ever since I came back from college.'

Georgia stepped into the doorway as, in one stride, Jarrod was beside his stepmother. His arms reached out for her, dragged her to him, and to Georgia's horror Jarrod began to kiss the older woman. When he released her they stood close together, as still as marble statues.

CHAPTER NINE

'JARROD?' Georgia's eyes went to his tortured face. 'Aunt Isabel? What—? I can't—' She swallowed convulsively. 'Jarrod?' Her voice broke and the pain in her chest made her clutch at the doorframe.

Isabel's face seemed to turn a shade paler. But not as waxen as Jarrod's.

'Georgia,' he said thinly, 'how long have you been there?'

'Really, Georgia.' Isabel found her voice. 'You had no right to skulk around listening to a private conversation.'

'Didn't she, Isabel?' Jarrod retorted bitterly. 'Hell! I need a drink.'

He crossed to the bar and leant over the top, jerkily grasping a bottle of Scotch and splashing some unsteadily into a glass, downing the liquid in one gulp. As Georgia and his stepmother watched him he stared broodingly into the empty tumbler, went to refill it and stopped. He set the bottle back on the bar with a thud before furiously throwing the glass against the bricks of the large open fireplace in the side-wall.

Georgia jumped as the shattering sound seemed to snap her out of her stricken immobility. Jarrod had kissed her aunt, his own stepmother.

'Georgia, I think you should go home,' her aunt said. 'This isn't the time. It's a family affair.'

Georgia didn't even glance at her; her eyes were on Jarrod. She watched a multitude of expressions cross his face, some so fleetingly that she was unable to put a name to them. But there was disbelief, hurt, and pain—deep, desolate pain—beneath his anger. Then all the fight seemed to go out of him, leaving his eyes empty of emotion.

'A family affair?' He regarded his stepmother levelly. 'And Georgia isn't family?'

'Jarrod, don't—'

'No.' He spoke flatly. 'Leave us, Isabel. As you pointed out, Georgia and I have to talk.'

Isabel's hand fluttered undecidedly to her throat. 'Don't you think it would be best to leave it until tomorrow?' she suggested, but Jarrod shook his head.

'No. Tonight. Leave us alone, Isabel.'

Still the older woman hesitated, and then, with lips set in a thin, disapproving line, she left the room. In the final, swift glance she afforded her niece Georgia was sure she saw a moment's apprehension. But all Georgia's attention returned to Jarrod, and the lengthening silence almost choked her as she held her breath, gazing bewilderedly at him.

She felt as though her whole world had shattered about her, falling into a million agonising pieces. Jarrod and her aunt?

He crossed the room towards her and she put out her hand as if to ward him off. But she needn't have worried, for he stopped some distance from her, his strong jaw clenched.

'Georgia, we have to talk. Sit down. Please.'

'I don't think there's anything that has to be said,' she got out flatly.

'How much did you hear?'

'Hear? I didn't need to hear anything. What I saw was enough. I can't believe you—'

'Georgia, don't.' He stopped and ran a hand through his hair. 'There's more to it than—'

It was her turn to bite off a desolate laugh. 'I don't see how there could be.' Pain clutched at her, icy tentacles wrapping around her heart, squeezing, constricting. On leaden feet she shuffled backwards to a lounge chair, subsiding onto the edge of it, her back tensely straight, her hands clasped together to still their trembling. 'How could you?' she asked huskily. 'How could you kiss Aunt Isabel like that?'

'Georgia, please? I'm trying to tell you it wasn't what you think—'

'You said you loved me.'

'I did. I do. But…' He looked at her with uncharacteristic indecision before his expression suddenly hardened. 'I have to go away,' he said abruptly.

Georgia's tongue-tip moistened her dry lips but no words came out.

'I'm going to the States.' His eyes met hers, only to slide immediately away. 'I need to see my father.'

'I thought he was in Hong Kong,' Georgia said carefully.

'He's going on to the States. There's something I want—I have to talk to him about.'

With a wave of despair Georgia put her hands over her mouth. If she didn't get out of the room she'd be sick. Jarrod and her aunt? No! 'Are you going to tell him about… about…tonight?'

'No! I was going anyway,' Jarrod was saying. 'I was going to tell you. Something's come up. There's a problem over there.' Still he didn't look at her.

Her heart thumped inside her chest so loudly that it deafened her. She swallowed, feeling panic rising. He ran his hand discomposedly through his hair as he turned back to face her, his eyelashes falling to shield his expression. Then his jaw tensed and he seemed to draw himself up. 'I may not come back. I might have to take over the North American subsidiary of the company.'

Feeling flowed back into her body and she flinched with pain. He couldn't be saying this. He couldn't. This couldn't be happening. Not after all they'd been to each other. Were to each other.

Panic spread through her in pulsating waves. 'Jarrod, how could you do this?'

'Georgia, I'm sorry,' he said flatly. 'I never meant to hurt you.'

'No!' Georgia shook her head. 'No more lies! I have to go.' She stood up and her legs almost gave way beneath her.

Jarrod went to reach for her but she waved him away, couldn't bear him to touch her.

'Georgia!'

'No!' Georgia yelled at him. 'No! I hate you, Jarrod! I never believed I could hate anyone as much as I hate you at this moment. And hell will freeze over before I want to set eyes on you again. You or Aunt Isabel.'

A muscle near his mouth twitched edgily and he seemed to be having trouble relaxing the tension in his jaw. 'Georgia, I'm truly sorry it has to end this way. But things aren't the way they seem. God, I wonder if anything ever was,' he added bitterly. 'But, believe me, Georgia, I did love you.'

'Love? You don't know what the word means, Jarrod.' Tears stung her eyes and the pain in her chest increased, making her feel sure her heart was breaking.

'Oh, I know what it means,' he said quietly, and she laughed.

'You know what sex means and that's totally different. Well, because of you I know what sex is too. And I know what love isn't.' She walked towards the door.

'Georgia.' He went to touch her shoulder and she angrily shrugged him off.

'Don't touch me.' She hurled the vitriolic words at him. 'How could you do this, Jarrod? How could you use me like a—like a body? Any body?'

'I told you in the beginning we had to keep it light. I didn't intend things to go so far but you—'

'Oh! How gallant of you. So I led you on, forced you to make love to me.' She held up one shaking hand. 'No, I'll rephrase that. I made you have sex with me.'

'I didn't mean... You're very attractive, desirable... Georgia, you were willing and I'm just a man.'

'No,' she sneered, agony lashing her. 'No, Jarrod, you're not a man. You don't know the meaning of that word either. You've got it all wrong. Real men don't do what you've done, what you're doing.'

His lips thinned and she suspected that her words had hurt him but she was beyond caring now. Inconceivable anguish engulfed her and she turned on her heel then and left him there, flying down the stairs, running through the darkness, unstoppable tears coursing down her face to blind her.

Georgia had felt as though her world had ended in those agonising moments four years ago. But that was only the tip of the iceberg, for that fateful pain-filled night had only just begun.

Jarrod stood up in a sharp, uncharacteristically graceless movement, almost upsetting the easy chair he'd been sitting on, and the sound brought Georgia back from that terrible night. In one sharp, shocking split second she was in the present again.

What had they been discussing? Songs. Her sexy song. And Jarrod's air of censure. Georgia wiped her hand shakily across her eyes as he took a couple of stiff-legged strides away from her, his back straight and so obviously reproachful. How dared he?

'Are you short of money, Georgia?' he asked, and she blinked, taken totally by surprise by his question.

'Short of...? No, of course not. What made you ask that?'

'Lockie told me about your car and I thought if you're letting Lockie record these songs because you need the money then perhaps I could—'

'No!' How could he ever imagine she'd consider taking money from him? 'No, Jarrod, I don't need money at all.' The words came out from between her clenched teeth but before she could continue Lockie rejoined them, and even he had trouble drawing the other two into more than a semblance of conversation.

Not long after that Jarrod took his leave, and before Lockie could ask any questions Georgia escaped to her room to get dressed, exhausted and emotionally drained, as though she had been on an arduous journey and still had to face the formidable trek back.

The patrons of the club tonight were, like last night, a sympathetic audience, and Georgia had to admit that her brother had them eating out of his hand. He had the knack on stage of winning over the most apathetic of groups.

However, just at that moment, Georgia had her own smile plastered on her face. After her pain-filled reminiscences she was finding it almost impossible to relax tonight.

Usually after the first song her nerves had settled, and she could convince herself she was all but laid back by the time the halfway mark of the evening arrived. But not tonight. Tonight she was impossibly more uptight than she'd been in their opening number.

The reason for her nervousness was sitting at the same table in the front row. The hot spotlights that lit the stage had a tendency to cloak the rest of the room in shadow, but no matter how hard she tried Georgia couldn't block out the sight of Jarrod's tall body lounging back in his chair as he listened to the music.

He hadn't mentioned that he was coming to the show again tonight. Last night had been bad enough but to have him here for this performance, tonight of all nights, was almost more than she could bear.

He was sitting with no outward signs of discomposure, totally unaware of the havoc he was creating within Georgia as she waited to sing the song. Her song.

It's just a song, she kept telling herself, and she wasn't going to allow herself to continue being such a coward.

Her heartbeats raced and her legs felt jelly-like and decidedly weak. Would it never end, this wild, breathless yearning that continued to war with the hurt and hatred that had simmered deep inside her for the past four years? And that had nothing to do with a song.

'Now for the icing on the cake, the pièce de résistance.' Lockie stepped up to the microphone again. 'This will be the title song from the album we hope to cut, and when you hear it you'll understand why we chose this song. It's a sizzler.' He ran his finger around the inside of his collar and fanned himself exaggeratedly. 'Ladies and gentlemen, I give you the incredible, the dynamic Georgia Grayson.'

Lockie stepped back and the band began to play the softly seductive introduction. The lights dimmed, one warm spot enveloping Georgia as she stood in the silky, shimmering midnight-blue dress that clung where it touched her body. She knew it set off her faintly tanned shoulders, moulded her breasts, nipped in at the waist, to fall with soft sensuality over her hips and swirl about her nylon-clad legs. Her high-heeled shoes were little more than thin criss-crossed straps, and she hadn't needed Lockie's low whistle when she'd appeared on stage to tell her she looked her best.

Now she had to sing the song. She kept telling herself that if anything was going to exorcise the past singing this song would do it. It was all very well for Lockie to have been ecstatic when she'd changed her mind about singing it. But now the time had come… Could she?

It was sexy, perhaps suggestive—the words, the evocative score written while the afterglow of lovemaking had still carried her high. And Jarrod was here, not feet from her. She was unable to prevent her gaze from sliding across to where he sat. She knew intuitively that his eyes were fastened on her and she nervously raised one hand to push back a strand of her hair, shining like ebony in the spotlight.

Was he sitting just a little straighter now, some thread of tension running through him?

And then she was singing.

'Touch me, touch my body…'

The noise from the audience seemed to cease immediately.

'Touch me, let your fingers brush me...'

Not a sliver of ice tinkled in a glass.

'Can you feel the fire start...?'

Georgia sang instinctively from verse to chorus, her voice catching, throbbing the enticing lyrics, bringing the words to life with spellbinding expression.

'In my dreams I've felt that fire...'

She could so easily let that blaze flare, just knowing he was there.

'Your fingers setting me aflame...'

So vividly she remembered the exquisite pleasure of Jarrod's hands moving over her.

'Finding every sensuous secret...'

He knew each erotic place, every tiny hidden part of her, and he knew how to drive her far beyond all control.

'As I softly sigh your name...'

Oh, Jarrod.

'Touch me, touch my body...'

She sang to him. For him.

It was impossible to read his expression from the stage but she was so physically aware of him that the rest of the audience faded into the dimness, might not have been there at all. She was alone with Jarrod and the years slipped away. He was her first love, her only lover. Her voice reached out to him, caressed him the way she used to, the way he used to.

'Touch me, our bodies one at last...'

Oh, Jarrod, touch me, her heart cried out as her voice faded away.

Georgia was numb now and oblivious to the audience's response. As the last note died away there was a spine-tingling cluster of seconds of total silence before everyone was standing, hands clapping, crying for more.

The deafening sound started to seep through Georgia's anaesthetised state, startling her, and for a moment she was disorientated, barely aware of her surroundings or her actions. She sensed Lockie moving beside her as the house lights rose.

He reached up, his hand covering the microphone, and spoke softly in her ear.

'Bloody hell, Georgia. That was something else.'

Georgia scarcely heard him as she blinked, refocusing on Jarrod. He was leaning forward in his seat now and in the hazy light through the faint drift of cigarette smoke his face looked deathly pale. He had the stilled, pained appearance of a man who'd been dealt a sharp, unexpected blow to the solar plexus and couldn't quite regain his breath.

'You'd better say thanks,' Lockie prompted, indicating the still cheering crowd, and Georgia struggled to draw herself together.

She pasted her smile a trifle shakily onto her face. 'I need a break, Lockie,' she said in a low voice, dropping her head forward so that no one could read her lips.

'OK. But they'll want you to sing again later,' he warned from behind her. 'Be back when we finish ''Mona Lisa's Lost her Smile''.'

Georgia nodded. She was having difficulty getting the message through to her legs to carry her.

'OK?' he repeated, and she nodded again, turning away, somehow getting herself off the stage.

'A big hand for the fantastic Georgia Grayson.' Lockie made a flourishing bow after her. 'Who shall, I assure you, return.'

Georgia almost fell into the small cubicle she used for a dressing room. She struggled over to open the high-level hopper window, to stand leaning against the wall, gulping in the faint breath of fresh air that filtered inside. Through the opening of the window she could see a couple of stars twinkling in the dark sky and she swallowed painfully.

She felt drained, as though a whole emotion-laden segment of her life had been committed to film and the reel had been rerun before her eyes. Warts and all. All the joy. All the exultation. Then all the pain.

There was no way she would be able to sing that song again.

So much for banishing her ghosts! It had ripped her apart, torn open sensitive lesions. And it had all happened in full view of the public. She groaned weakly. One particular member of the public. She'd bared her very essence to Jarrod Maclean.

And she'd been so transparent. A moan of pain escaped her raw throat. Transparent? When it came to Jarrod she was as clear as crystal. Yet oh, so brittle. Hadn't she showed that four years ago? So now he'd know she hadn't changed.

She hadn't; she knew that now. She still loved him as much as she had back then. Regardless of what he'd done.

It's physical, she told herself again, purely physical. Georgia sighed with despair. She'd given up trying to believe that. Physical. Emotional. Seventeen or seventy. Jarrod Maclean had taken her heart and it was his for always, to cherish or to shatter.

But he didn't deserve it!

Georgia felt like crying but the lump in her throat was threatening to choke her, seemed to be lodged there, the relief of tears denied her. Her entire body ached and she shakily pushed herself away from the wall, her gaze still unseeingly on the dark sky, her shoulders sagging.

Jarrod was right. She'd always known she didn't have the temperament to be a performer. She lacked that certain something that Lockie and the other boys possessed—their pleasure at being on stage, their elation from the applause. She was a behind-the-scenes person. She could write the songs, but...

Georgia sighed brokenly. It was all so clear now. She'd allowed herself to drift along these past four years. She'd meandered through life like a slow-flowing stream, choosing the path of least resistance. All the fight had been drained out of her and she'd never attempted to replenish it.

In a flash of revelation she recognised that she hadn't really been living but merely existing, going from day to day, week to week. Morgan had been right about that.

Had Jarrod been responsible for that too? No, it was entirely her own fault. She'd put too much faith in him, literally placed her life, her happiness in his hands, and when he'd decided he wanted his own life, excluding her, she'd let herself sink into herself. Eating. Sleeping. Breathing. But not living.

But she couldn't forgive him for what he'd done, could she? The hurt ran too deeply. She sighed again—a long, broken sound that echoed in the small room. And then she caught her breath, sensing she was no longer alone. She spun around.

He was leaning with one shoulder against the doorjamb, to all appearances filling the door space.

In that first, wide-eyed glance she took in the whole heart-stopping length of him. From the top of his head, his thick and vital dark hair, to his toes, cased in cream trainers.

He wore a short-sleeved pale apricot tailored cotton shirt, open at the neck, the colour accentuating the tan of the V of skin showing where the collar was unbuttoned, the shirt matched with a pair of light cream canvas jeans in the latest fashion style. His hands were in his deep pockets and one ankle was crossed over the other in a composed, casual pose.

Yet Georgia knew instinctively that he was anything but relaxed. In that first glance she was unequivocally aware of the cord of tension that ran through him, holding his body taut. A pulse beat in one smoothly shaven cheek and his blue eyes were sapphire-bright. Georgia suspected that the hands in his pockets were balled into fists.

Dear heaven! It wasn't over yet.

'Are you all right?' His easy words startled her and her lips slackened, a captured breath escaping in a soft hiss.

Georgia gathered herself together with some difficulty. 'Why?' She could have bitten her tongue. Why indeed?

'You left the stage in something of a rush.'

Georgia shrugged. 'I found the lights particularly hot and needed a break.'

Jarrod raised one dark eyebrow.

'It's quite exhausting really,' Georgia elaborated.

'Especially when you put so much into it.'

Her eyes fell and she shrugged again. 'That's what I'm paid to do.'

He was silent at that and Georgia looked up guardedly.

'Did you have to wipe yourself out the way you did tonight?'

She gazed back at him, unable to find a quick rejoinder.

'Whatever they pay you, it's not nearly enough.' He pushed himself upright and made a point of looking around the small dressing room. At her make-up case, the hard chair, the mirror with the harsh little fluorescent tube over it, at her change of clothes hanging on the rough hook on the wall.

'They pay me pretty well actually,' Georgia said quickly. 'A nice little sum to put towards my new car.'

Jarrod was watching her with hooded eyes. 'Remember what I said about the merry-go-round, and how you might not be able to get off? And so it starts.'

'As you know from firsthand experience,' Georgia gibed, and he took his hands out of his pockets and rested them on his hips.

'Yes, since you remember so well,' he tossed back at her.

Remember? Oh, there was nothing wrong with her memory. But what about his?

'It's hardly any of your business, Jarrod.' Georgia's chin lifted angrily.

'Perhaps it isn't, but someone should tell you you're burning yourself out.'

'Based on your viewing of only two performances?' Georgia remarked sarcastically. The way she felt at the moment she suspected she was already burnt out, but she wasn't going to have him tell her that.

'I'm just concerned that Lockie's going to try to talk you into doing more shows. You won't be able to keep up the pace, Georgia. Two nights a week here on top of your full-time job, plus the hours you spend practising, not to mention your study.' He raised his hands and let them fall. 'And for what? It's too much.'

'I'm simply helping Lockie out,' she told him defiantly. 'Mandy will be back next week.'

Jarrod said something under his breath and took a step into the room, making the cubby-hole seem even smaller than it was.

'And can this Mandy sing as well as you do?'

'Better.'

'I find that hard to believe. Look, Georgia. Lockie—' he began, and then stopped, shaking his head. 'We've been through all this before too, Georgia. I'm worried about your health. Look at yourself in the mirror.'

'What's that supposed to mean?'

'It means there's shadows beneath your eyes and you've lost weight.'

Georgia's lips twisted. She'd lost a good fourteen pounds in four years. Or rather, in a month four years ago. She'd just never regained it. 'My puppy fat, you mean. I thought thin was fashionable. Anyway, I'd say you couldn't talk about that. You've lost weight yourself.'

'We're not discussing me. And you know very well what I mean, Georgia. Don't make yourself ill over this.'

Ill! she wanted to taunt him. No, not ill, Jarrod, just sick at heart.

She glanced up at him with fire in her eyes and the concern on his face was almost her undoing. She very nearly threw herself into his arms. But she stopped herself, hardening herself.

It was too late for him to be concerned about her. But she must keep this conversation light, she told herself, or she'd end up making a fool of herself all over again.

'Ill? I'm as healthy as a horse.'

He gave a short, sharp laugh. 'Healthy or not, you were nearly dropping when you finished that song.'

'It was that kind of song,' she quipped lightly, and his lips thinned.

'It was that,' he agreed drily, and Georgia shifted indifferently. 'It was pretty sexy.'

Georgia's smile didn't reach her eyes. 'So Lockie and the boys say.'

'But that song—it just seems a little out of character somehow.'

'Does it?' How she wished she had the aplomb to add a comeback with a conviction of truth. 'That's not what I've been told', with a provocative smirk. Or perhaps, 'I could name a dozen guys who'd give me the seal of sexy approval'. But she couldn't. She wasn't outrageous and there had only been one...

'Still, Lockie thought your song would be the best one to feature on the album, and unfortunately I can see his point.' He paused and his eyes flickered. 'It *is* brilliant.'

'Thanks.' Georgia raised her chin.

He was still gazing at her with a tense inscrutability and she felt an urge to shock him, make him see her as he once had, remind him...

'I wrote it four years ago,' she added levelly.

He tensed and the shutters fell, shrouding his expression, but Georgia valiantly held his gaze, the taste of imminent revenge sweet on her tongue.

'As a matter of fact, I wrote it the night we first made love, so if it's the hit Lockie predicts it will be you'll deserve some of the credit.'

Georgia's heartbeats raced and part of her could have cringed in horror as she heard herself speak. She turned away, picking up her brush in an unsteady hand. Her mouth was dry as she pulled it unnecessarily through her hair.

Her eyes were drawn to his reflection in the mirror and what she saw had her hand halting, the brush poised above her head.

He was momentarily unaware that she could see him and his expression shocked her. He looked like a man who had been surprised by a massive punch—until he realised she had swung back to face him and recovered himself.

'Really?' he remarked offhandedly.

His seeming lack of reaction and uninterested tone convinced her she had imagined that fleeting glimpse of pain, and she mocked herself derisively for being a gullible fool.

'Well, you did make it memorable,' she said with equal indifference. 'I have to give credit where credit is due.'

A wash of colour darkened the ridge of his cheekbones and, sensing her advantage, Georgia lunged onwards.

'I remember it well. Don't they say a woman never forgets her first lover? But I suppose it's different for a man. With all the women who have come after me you've most probably forgotten.' Georgia could only be amazed at her outward calm.

'I remember, Georgia,' he said in a low voice, as though his throat hurt.

'You do? I'm impressed,' she jeered. 'Should I be flattered, hmm?'

Jarrod held up his hands. 'That's enough, Georgia, don't you think?'

'We're adults, Jarrod, aren't we? We enjoyed each other. What's more natural than that?'

'It wasn't like that.'

'Like what?'

'The way you're implying.'

'Wasn't it?'

'All right, Georgia. I don't need this moment of nostalgia right now,' he snapped brutally.

Georgia knew she had invited his cruelty, yet still her hurt drove her. 'Oh? Why not?'

'Because I don't.' His words were slivers of ice.

'Surely you're not embarrassed at being reminded of our rolls in the hay? Or should I say romps in the dry grass?'

Jarrod shoved his hands back into his pockets. 'Don't cheapen it, Georgia,' he said, and there was something in his tone that for a moment bothered her, but she refused to analyse it.

'I may be easy but I'm not cheap.' The saying rolled mockingly from her lips.

'Suppose we just drop this now?'

'You *are* embarrassed.' Her laugh didn't ring completely true in her ears and she swallowed as her heartbeats seemed to increase agitatedly. But Jarrod had turned away to leave her and her anger reintensified. 'Or is it something else?'

He stopped then, his back to her for long seconds before he slowly turned to face her again.

'Guilt, perhaps?' Georgia knew as soon as the words were out that she had gone too far and she stepped backwards, coming up against the chair.

'Are you intent on getting your pound of flesh, Georgia?' he ground out wryly. 'That's what this is all about, I take it?'

'Maybe it's just the truth.' Her voice held a little less conviction.

'Guilt!' he repeated, and laughed harshly as his hands reached out, grasped her arms, his fingers bruising the soft skin where they held her. 'So you think I feel guilty? You don't know the half of it, you little fool.'

'Jarrod, you're hurting me.' She tried to twist out of his grip but he held her fast, continuing as though he hadn't heard her speak.

'I know what you're trying to do, Georgia. You've been spoiling for it since I came back. But, believe me, it's not going to work. If you want revenge, believe me, you've had it. I've more than settled the account for what I did. And I don't intend to pay any more—not by having you goad me, anyway.'

While he spoke his hands on her arms relaxed a little and, as though against his will, his fingers slid downwards, now unconsciously caressing, and the sensations he created in her had her trembling, her fear of his anger forgotten. That long-dormant, well-remembered glow he'd already fanned that afternoon began to grow again inside her.

She must have made some sound for he glanced sharply down at her.

'For pity's sake, Georgia. Don't play your sexy games with me any more,' he said hoarsely.

Georgia's lips parted with involuntary provocation and her tongue-tip moistened her dry mouth.

Jarrod's blue eyes, dark and stormy, were locked on her lips, as though he was committing their quivering shape to memory.

Now her whole body was coming alive, each nerve-ending aroused, every sense tuned to his nearness, the never-forgotten fire beginning to thaw her, to warm, to flare, to rage through her. She lifted her hand to rest it gently along his jaw, moved her fingers to trace the outline of his mouth.

His body was rigid, and for a fragment of a second she thought she felt his lips move urgently against her palm. Then he had thrust her roughly from him.

'Leave it, Georgia, for both our sakes. Unless you want to take the consequences.' He drew a ragged breath and Georgia reached shakily for the support of the back of the chair.

His words cut through her and the old wounds bled, transporting her agonisingly back in time. She was that naïve, trusting, so-in-love nineteen-year-old again.

'Jarrod, please…' The appeal came from her heart.

'Georgia.' He closed his eyes, his face drawn. He raked his hand agitatedly through his hair and she saw the unsteadiness of it.

'Don't you want me, Jarrod?' She imagined she'd only thought the words but she must have voiced them, for he looked at her with haunted, hungry eyes.

'Want you?' His lips twisted with self-derisive contempt. 'Oh, yes, I want you, Georgia. That's one of the perverted jokes of my life.' The muscles in his throat worked and his eyes flinched as he looked down at her. 'I'll go on wanting you with every breath, till the day I die.'

CHAPTER TEN

IN RETROSPECT Georgia wouldn't be able to believe she'd actually gone back out on the stage that night, but she did. She managed to perform another half-dozen songs before the show drew to a close.

After his tortured admission Jarrod turned and left her alone in the dressing room. She stood transfixed, her eyes on the space where he'd been standing, and she would have sworn that her heartbeats had ceased altogether. She hung in limbo for indeterminate, unforgettable seconds.

Jarrod had admitted he wanted her. *Still wanted her.* Dear Lord, she groaned inwardly. And she still wanted him. So desperately.

Then reaction set in. Her senses soared and just as suddenly sank. There was something dreadfully wrong. If he still had some feeling for her then why weren't they at this moment locked in each other's arms, finding the rapture they'd once known? Why?

Wasn't he aware of the effect he still had on her? He must be. For all her antagonism towards him, he only had to touch her physically and she melted into him. He must have felt it too.

Her lips twisted as pain gripped her. So it appeared he'd turned his back on her again. What was it about her that could inspire a fiery desire and a cold rejection at one and the same time? It wasn't her fault, she told herself. Was she forgetting what had happened that night?

She stood aching with hurt and confusion. If she hadn't

forgiven him, how could she feel the way she did about him now? Then through the daze of bewilderment her subconscious recognised the sound of Country Blues playing the last song of the last set of numbers. She had to go back on stage. Lockie would reintroduce her and she had to be there, ready and waiting in the wings.

And somehow she was. She went through the motions of singing, the lyrics coming naturally, while her heart thudded painfully in her chest and her mind tossed over that dreadful scene. For when she'd stepped back into the spotlight the first face she'd seen in the audience had been Jarrod's.

She had assumed he would have left. It hadn't even occurred to her that he would stay for the rest of the show. But he sat the never-ending evening out.

Now, thankfully, it was over. People had gone and Georgia had escaped back to her dressing room, her body shivering as she imagined that she could sense Jarrod's presence still filling the small room.

Clumsily she stepped out of the blue dress and donned the loose black trousers and white blouse she'd worn up to the club. Then she removed her make-up, applying only a light moisturiser and just a touch of lipstick.

Her face looked pale after the severity of the stage make-up, wan and lifeless, except for two spots of high colour in her cheeks. She felt flushed and feverish and yearned desperately for bed and the oblivion of sleep.

No doubt Lockie would keep her waiting, and she had the beginnings of a headache, her stomach feeling decidedly fluttery.

When she entered the main entertainment room only Lockie and Andy were there. Evan and Ken had gone, and thankfully there was no sign of Jarrod.

'Georgia. At last.' Lockie caught sight of her and beckoned her over. 'We've been waiting for you. We want to make tracks,' he said, 'if we're taking in this party.'

Georgia turned her amazed gaze on her brother. 'You can't

be serious, Lockie.' She glanced at her wrist-watch. 'What party?'

'We met a group from one of our old gigs and they invited us to go along,' Lockie explained.

'The night's young, Georgia.' Andy grinned. 'Or should I say morning.'

'Well, I've got no intention of going to any party. I'm really tired.' She frowned at her brother. 'I wouldn't last the distance, I'm afraid. I'll take a taxi home.'

'I wonder if Jarrod wants to come?' Lockie looked around. 'Where is he?'

'Speak of the devil,' Andy muttered, and Georgia turned slightly to face the tall, broad-shouldered man striding across to join them.

'Are you ready to go?' he asked, his eyes flicking expressionlessly over Georgia before going back to Lockie.

Georgia could hear a strange ringing in her ears. This was a nightmare. The silence seemed to stretch, grow, echo loudly in the empty room. Did he expect—?

'How about you, Jarrod? Are you coming to the party?' Lockie asked, and Jarrod shook his head.

'At this time of night? I don't think so.'

'You're getting old, mate,' Andy teased. 'We have it on good authority that there will be a stack of good-looking birds there, and you're fancy-free, aren't you?'

Georgia did glance at Jarrod then, and his jaw was set, his face as though it were carved from stone, showing not a flicker of the amusement that Andy might have expected.

'I suppose I am,' he replied carefully. 'But I'll have to give it a miss tonight.'

'Then you can give Georgia a lift home,' said Lockie blandly.

'Ah!' Andy put his finger to his nose in an exaggerated pose of sudden revelation. 'I see.'

'I'm sure you do,' Jarrod said drily.

Georgia was frozen, quite beyond feeling, as she looked across at him.

He gave a crooked smile and, taking her arm, he headed her towards the door. 'We'll see you later. Have a good time.'

'I'm sorry about that.' Georgia eventually made herself speak. They had been travelling in silence and were about halfway home when she finally had control of herself enough to volunteer her apology for Andy's lack of tact. 'Andy can be something of a joker.'

'It doesn't matter.' Jarrod's voice mirrored his lack of interest and he drove on in that same heavy silence, accelerating their speed a little, as though he was in a hurry to be home.

And shot of her, Georgia mused wryly. After her behaviour in the dressing room who could blame him? she had to concede.

'I'm sorry about before, too,' she began, and he frowned.

'For what?'

'For baiting you. Earlier, in my dressing room.'

'Forget it, Georgia,' he said wearily.

She couldn't, she wanted to cry out. She couldn't forget it, not the last bit anyway.

'I behaved abominably.'

'Look, Georgia, let's not hold a post-mortem. Shall we simply say we both got a little het up and overreacted?'

'But—'

'Georgia, I'm tired. And so are you. Let's just get home and forget the whole evening. I already have.'

And had he forgotten so effortlessly what he'd said? 'I want you, Georgia.' Looking at his set profile, the way his hands gripped the steering wheel, feeling the tension emanating from him, Georgia rather doubted it would be that easy for either of them to pretend that that emotion-charged scene had never happened. They'd have to talk about it if they were going to see as much of each other as they had been doing. The dull throb at Georgia's temples grew more intense, and she was as relieved as he most definitely was to see the lights of home.

*   *   *

Two days later Georgia received a telephone call at work and she hurried to answer it. Who could it be? The family knew she wasn't suppose to have private calls unless it was an emergency. Her heart skipped a beat with dread. What could have happened? She swallowed nervously. 'Hello?'

'Georgia. It's me, Andy. Now don't panic.'

'Andy, what is it?' Mr Johns, the manager of the bookshop, was frowning at Georgia across the workroom, and she lowered her head.

'We've had a bit of a—well…' Andy paused. 'Something's happened.'

'What? It's not my father, is it?' She gripped the receiver tensely.

'No, he's fine,' Andy reassured her quickly. 'It's the house. We've had a fire and—'

'A fire?' Georgia repeated, oblivious now of the interested faces of her workmates. 'You mean the house has burned down?'

'No. Nothing like that. Just the kitchen bit.'

'The kitchen… Andy, you'd better start at the beginning.'

'It's all under control now,' Andy placated her. 'I mean, I'm ringing from the house, so that should prove it's not all that bad. But do you think you could come home, Georgia? Lockie's running around like a stunned mullet, being a bit ineffectual, or, at least, he was until Jarrod arrived and took charge.'

'Jarrod's there?' Georgia repeated faintly. Not again. Was he always going to be coming to their rescue?

'He was. He heard the sirens and came over. But he should be at the bookshop any minute now. He's going to drive you home.'

Georgia groaned. 'Oh, Andy. Why did you bother him? Why couldn't Lockie come?'

'Are you kidding, Georgia? He's a genius with music but as a fearless firefighter even he'd be the first to admit he leaves a lot to be desired. I wouldn't exactly trust him to drive just yet.' Andy chuckled. 'As a matter of fact I was coming to get you, but Jarrod insisted he bring you home.'

Was there a question in Andy's tone? 'Much more and I'll have to pay him award rates for chauffeuring,' Georgia muttered, and he laughed.

'True. What a pity he's your cousin, Georgia. I'd say there'd be women who'd kill to be chauffeured anywhere by him. You girls go for those rugged good looks, don't you?'

'You're telling the story, Andy,' Georgia quipped drily, and looked up to see Jarrod talking to Mr Johns, while the female assistants seemed unable to take their eyes off their visitor. 'Jarrod's here now, Andy, so I'd better go. See you soon.' She hung up and hurried across the room.

'Mr Johns, I'm sorry I—' she began apologetically.

'Now don't you worry, Miss Grayson.' He waved his hand grandly. 'Mr Maclean has explained the situation to me and of course you must go home and lend a hand. I trust all will be as well as can be expected.'

'That's very kind of you, Mr Johns. I'll make up the time off,' Georgia assured him, but he brushed that aside with very unusual good humour.

'Don't give that a thought, Miss Grayson. We'll see you tomorrow unless we hear to the contrary.'

'Thank you.' Georgia's eyes flicked to Jarrod and away again.

'No need to thank me. Now, off you go. Don't keep Mr Maclean waiting.'

Georgia hurried off to get her bag and returned to follow Jarrod out through the shop.

'Georgia?' Jodie's voice from behind a shelf halted her. 'Sorry to hear about the fire. I hope there's not too much damage done.' Jodie's eyes were on the man standing beside Georgia and Georgia was forced to make the introductions.

'Jodie, this is my cousin, Jarrod Maclean. Jarrod, meet Jodie Craig.'

'Hi!' Jodie held out her hand and smiled broadly. 'I'm glad

you're not my cousin,' she added outrageously, and Jarrod laughed. 'How come you've kept him such a secret, Georgia?'

'I've been overseas,' Jarrod told her easily, his eyes dancing.

'Then welcome back.' Jodie wasn't trying to conceal her interest and Georgia managed to find her voice.

'Shouldn't we be going, Jarrod?' she said somewhat sharply, and felt herself flush as Jodie's smile widened knowingly.

'I get the message, Georgia.' She grimaced good-naturedly. 'See you tomorrow. And nice to have met you, Jarrod.'

They continued out to the car and Georgia forced herself to put Jodie and her comments out of her mind. 'How bad is it?' she asked as Jarrod set the car in motion.

'Not too bad. It could have been disastrous, though, if Andy hadn't acted so quickly.'

'Is Lockie all right?'

Jarrod laughed softly, the sound running over Georgia like a feather's touch, teasing her senses. 'Sure. Just a trifle bewildered.'

'Do they know what happened?'

'Faulty wiring in the kitchen, they think. Andy and Lockie were downstairs and smelled the smoke. They found the wall at the back of the kitchen ablaze.'

Georgia closed her eyes. What if no one had been at home?

'The fire brigade was on the scene pretty quickly but even so the back of the house was well alight by the time they arrived. Fortunately they were able to contain the fire in that section but there's some water damage to the bedrooms on the right side of the house.'

Georgia rubbed her eyes tiredly. What more could happen? And why had it all started with Jarrod's return?

'We can be thankful there was no wind today,' he said, and shot a glance at her pale face. 'It's not too drastic, Georgia. It can be repaired.'

She nodded. 'It's not… It's just that everything seems to be happening at once at the moment—going wrong. This trouble with Morgan, Lockie and Mandy, and—' She stopped.

'And?' he queried.

'Just everything,' she finished flatly. And his coming home. That was the worst. It took away her self-possession, her ability to cope.

Her gaze was drawn sideways. His return. Oh, Jarrod, she wanted to cry. Didn't he sometimes remember those days, those passion-filled nights? Didn't outrageously sensual thoughts torture him the way they did her?

She tore her eyes from him, from his tanned hands on the steering wheel, from the fine dark hair on his arms, from the bulge of firm muscle emerging from the short sleeves of his soot-stained shirt. She had to ignore the physical fascination, the erotic scent of him, the faint smell of smoke that still clung to him.

'How's Uncle Peter?' she asked, her voice all but steady.

'Not so good today. I'd been home at lunchtime to check on him; that's how I came to hear the sirens.' He sighed. 'He had a bad night last night. I thought...' He stopped and shrugged. 'Perhaps if he were younger the doctors might attempt operating, but they say he'd never survive surgery.'

They turned onto the access road leading past the Graysons' house just as the fire engine drove away. Georgia caught her breath. The front of the house looked surprisingly untouched but when Jarrod swung into the driveway the evidence of the fire could be seen in black scorch marks and peeling paint along the side past Georgia's bedroom window.

Lockie and Andy walked around from the back of the house as they climbed from the car. Both men were soot-streaked and dishevelled and Lockie pulled a wry face at his sister as they stood surveying the damage.

'Looks worse than it is, Georgia,' he told her. 'At least all our equipment is at the club so we didn't have to worry about that.'

'Just like you to think of your stuff first, Lockie.' Andy

gave him a shove. 'I'm sure Georgia is more concerned about the refrigerator and stove, aren't you, Georgia?'

'And I suppose your concern about the fridge doesn't have anything to do with food, does it, mate?' Lockie remarked shrewdly. 'At least they're insured.'

'You mean your gear isn't?' Jarrod frowned and Lockie gave him a sheepish look.

'Some of it. What we could afford to insure.'

Jarrod shook his head but Georgia was barely listening to their conversation. The panes of glass in every window on this side of the house were broken and charcoal and smoke stains stretched along the weatherboard walls. She dreaded to think of the state that would confront her inside.

'The other side and the front of the house are untouched,' Jarrod said quietly. 'It will mean quite an extensive rebuild at the back but it's not irreparable.'

'Did you phone Dad and tell him, Lockie?' Georgia asked her brother, and he nodded.

'While Jarrod was picking you up. And I rang the insurance company. The assessors are coming out tomorrow. They said we'd get priority, but that could mean anything or nothing.'

'Is Dad coming home?'

'No.' Lockie shook his head. 'He can't do anything here yet anyway so he decided he may as well finish the job he's working on. He reckons on two weeks at the most. By then the insurance company should have sorted the paperwork out and he can start the repairs here.' Lockie sighed. 'What a hell of a mess.'

'At least we can make the place secure.' Jarrod slapped him sympathetically on the back. 'There's some timber down by the back fence. We can board up the broken windows and the doorway between the kitchen and the rest of the house.' He strode towards the stack of wood. 'Come on, Lockie, let's get started.'

Andy and Georgia went upstairs, and even though Georgia was prepared she was still taken aback at the sight that met their eyes in the bedrooms. The beds and carpets were sodden and the acrid smell of smoke hung in the air, clinging to the curtains and covers.

'Where do we start?' Georgia asked, wrinkling her nose as the carpet squelched beneath her feet.

'Pile up the wet bedding, I guess,' Andy suggested, 'and drag the mattresses outside to dry.'

Georgia turned and tugged at a mattress.

'Don't go trying to lift that by yourself,' Andy admonished. 'You'll do yourself an injury and ruin any chance of having little Georgias running around.'

Georgia paused, her back to Andy, and she drew a steadying breath. A voice from the past rose to taunt her. Their family doctor's deep tones: 'She's a lucky young lady. There was no damage done so there's no reason why there can't be little dark-haired poppets in time to come.'

Andy gave no sign that he noticed her silence as they worked on together, laying out mattress and pillows on the lawn. They would have to get professional people to clean and dry them—and the carpets.

'Andy! Georgia!' Lockie called from the side of the house. 'Can you come and help hand up the timber?'

'Seems like us general dogsbodies are in great demand.' Andy laughed, slipping an arm about Georgia as they walked around to where Jarrod and Lockie had built a scaffold out of trestles and planks.

'Just pass up those bits.' Lockie pointed from his position on one side of the window as he wielded a hammer in his other hand.

'Lucky the window-panes are already broken,' Andy murmured to Georgia, and despite herself she had to smile.

But the smile on her lips faltered and died when her eyes met Jarrod's as he stood on the plank beside her brother. He was far too gorgeous, far too impossibly attractive, and she wanted to feel the security of his strong arms around her far too much. Then his eyes slid coldly, measuringly to where Andy's hand still rested on Georgia's shoulder.

'Do you need both of us?' she asked a little abruptly. 'If not I can drive down to the Laundromat and make a start on the wet sheets and blankets.'

'There's no need to go to the Laundromat.' Jarrod looked down on her from the scaffold. 'We'll take them over to my place later.'

'But there's stacks to wash and then dry and—'

'No matter. Mrs Pringle can fix them up.'

Georgia glared up at him then. 'We can't do that. Your father's housekeeper has enough to do without dumping all this extra work on her. I can easily take the van down to the Laundromat.'

Jarrod's jaw tightened but he made no comment as he turned with obvious restraint to hammer a piece of timber over the window.

'Can I have the keys, Lockie?' she asked her brother.

'Typical Georgia,' he muttered. 'Always independent.'

'It's not a matter of being independent, Lockie. I just feel it's our responsibility, not Mrs Pringle's. Now, can I have the keys, please?'

'Won't do you any good.' Lockie shrugged. 'The van's out of petrol. Andy was going down to get some on his bike before the fire broke out.'

Georgia glowered at her brother, too angry for words, and before she could find any the sound of a car slithering to a halt on the gravel verge outside distracted her.

A car door slammed, then the engine revved as the car left, and Morgan walked around the side of the house to stop, mouth agape, as she saw the results of the fire.

'What on earth happened?' she got out, obviously shocked.

'A fire this morning,' Lockie told her.

'It looks awful.' Morgan silently inspected the back of the house and then rejoined them to gaze up at the broken windows. 'Are our rooms all charred inside? And what about our clothes?'

'Just wet,' Georgia assured her.

'But—' She raised her arms and let them fall. 'Where are we going to sleep tonight, then? Not in there, that's for sure.'

'Oh, no.' Georgia was filled with dismay. 'I hadn't given that a thought. We won't be able to sleep in our rooms.'

'Not likely,' Morgan put in sarcastically. 'Gross!'

'All taken care of,' Lockie declared. 'We worked it all out before you came home, Georgia. Andy and I can camp out here, keep an eye on things.'

'And what about us?' Morgan demanded. 'If you think I'm—'

'You're coming to stay up at my place.' Jarrod's voice came evenly from the scaffold above them. 'You...' He paused slightly before adding, 'And Georgia.'

CHAPTER ELEVEN

'YOU'RE coming to stay up at my place.' Georgia could still feel the rush of shocked reaction she'd experienced as Jarrod had announced they would be staying at his home until their fire-damaged house could be repaired.

And she hadn't been able to extricate herself from the situation either. Both Lockie and Jarrod had pushed her protestations aside. To make it worse Morgan had then decided to bunk in with friends, so only Georgia had been forced to take advantage of Jarrod's hospitality.

Georgia wasn't alone in her dislike of the circumstances. Aunt Isabel, her lips thinned, was even less impressed with the idea of having her niece foisted upon her household. And for once Georgia felt that her aunt was well within her rights in complaining to Jarrod that, with his father being so ill, having visitors wasn't exactly convenient.

But Jarrod firmly overrode his stepmother as well, saying that his father's rooms were on the other side of the large house and that Peter wouldn't even be aware they had a guest.

However, Uncle Peter's nurse, an open, chatty woman, had told her patient about the fire and he insisted on the entire Grayson family moving in with him until their house was habitable again, only settling when he was told that Georgia was ensconced under his roof.

Georgia soon took to slipping in to see him each morning and evening before and after work, and he was quite obviously delighted to see her.

At least, she'd told herself as she'd dressed to go to work

that first morning, she would see little of Jarrod. He left for
the office much earlier than she did and she could avoid him
in the evening. So she'd risen and dressed, visited her uncle,
and walked unwarily through to the large, old-fashioned dining room. Jarrod had been sitting unconcernedly reading the
newspaper, a steaming cup of coffee in his hand.

'Good morning.'

Georgia's voice had failed her and she'd nodded an acknowledgement of his greeting.

Alone with him in the dining room, his hair still darkly
damp from his shower, the tantalising scent of his musky aftershave lotion overshadowing the aroma of freshly made coffee, it was far too close, too intimate.

Fortunately the housekeeper had entered the room at that
moment, for Georgia's throat had closed at her wayward
thoughts—thoughts of Jarrod and their being together for ever,
every morning. And at night.

Jarrod's eyes had rested on her as the housekeeper had tut-
tutted when Georgia refused all but tea and toast. Then she'd
returned to the kitchen and Georgia and Jarrod had been alone
again.

'I thought you would have already left for the office,'
Georgia ventured into the thick silence, hoping her tone was
more natural than it sounded in her ears. She slid a glance at
him. Had his lips tightened momentarily before he replied?

'Not today. I'll give you a lift to the bookshop.'

Georgia paused with her teacup halfway to her mouth. 'You
don't have to do that. It's out of your way.'

'Only by ten minutes or so.'

'At least twenty minutes,' she contradicted.

His eyes held hers for long, breath-stealing seconds before
he shrugged. 'Ten. Twenty. Who's counting?'

Georgia had gone to protest but something in the jut of his
square jaw, in the hard blue chips glittering in his eyes had
held her silent, and she'd finished her toast, forcing each bite
down with sips of tea.

For the next two mornings—yesterday and today—he had breakfasted with her, dropping her at work and then continuing on to his office. Only tight self-control prevented Georgia from groaning out loud when she thought of Jodie's teasing innuendoes about what she referred to as Georgia's 'hunky chauffeur'.

And now tonight, the first night that she'd worked a late shift, he'd been there at the bookshop to collect her, and Georgia could only pray that the repairs to their house would be completed in double-quick time. A tense sort of silence engulfed them as they drove along the dark road, past the damaged Grayson house and on to Jarrod's.

Every light in the house seemed to be burning. Jarrod swung the station wagon around the curve of the driveway, the headlights illuminating the sleek lines of the family doctor's Mercedes.

Georgia sat forward in her seat. 'Oh, no. Your father, Jarrod,' she breathed as he drew to a halt, and they both stumbled from the car.

Jarrod took the front steps two at a time and Georgia hurried to follow him. Isabel must have heard their arrival because she met them in the hallway.

'Your father took another bad turn,' she told Jarrod bluntly.

'When?'

'About two hours ago.'

'Two hours?' Jarrod repeated through his clenched teeth. 'Why didn't you get in touch with me? You knew I was at the office.'

'There didn't seem to be any point. There was nothing you could have done,' Isabel replied evenly.

'Only been here.' Jarrod moved towards the door.

'The doctor's with him, Jarrod. He's in a coma. He won't recognise you.'

Jarrod left them without commenting.

'How bad is it?' Georgia asked her aunt, marvelling at the older woman's self-possession.

Isabel shrugged. 'A matter of time.'

'Oh, no. Aunt Isabel, I'm sorry.' Georgia moved towards her aunt, only to stop as Isabel drew herself up, the small movement conveying to Georgia that she didn't want or need any sympathy or support. 'Poor Uncle Peter,' Georgia murmured. 'May I go in to see him?'

'As I told Jarrod, he won't even know you're there.' Isabel turned away and Georgia slowly continued down the hall towards her uncle's suite.

Peter Maclean died the next morning without regaining consciousness and the funeral was arranged for the following Tuesday. With dry eyes Isabel took over most of the arrangements. Georgia was sure the older woman would break down under the strain. But she didn't.

Jarrod also seemed to be coping extremely well with his father's death, and the funeral service, which was held in the local church, filled the old brick building to a rarely known capacity. Peter had had many friends, some even journeying interstate to pay their last respects. Many stayed at the Maclean home and there was much coming and going, with Isabel presiding like a dowager queen.

Georgia's father came down, returning to his job the next day. While he was home Geoff Grayson assessed the damage to their house and assured Georgia and Lockie he would have finished his contract in Caloundra within the week. Then he could turn his hand to repairing their own, fire-damaged house.

On the morning after the funeral—Wednesday, and Georgia's rostered day off from the bookshop—she found Jarrod in his father's study, going through Peter's papers. Isabel had gone into town to have lunch with friends.

'Do you need any help?' she offered hesitantly as she hovered uncertainly in the doorway.

Jarrod shook his head. He looked tired and drawn now that it was all over and Georgia could see that the ordeal of the past few days had taken its toll of him.

'There's not that much to do really. Everything's in order, as the saying goes.' He grimaced. 'Peter's known for some time how ill he was so he quite literally got his affairs sorted out, and that's making things easier for me.'

He sighed exhaustedly and Georgia took a step into the room. 'Would you like a cup of coffee? Mrs Pringle's just made some.'

'That would be great.' He looked at the antique wall clock. 'I can't seem to remember when I last ate.'

'I'll just go and get it.' Georgia went to the kitchen, poured his coffee, and added a plate of Mrs Pringle's sandwiches to the tray before returning to the study.

'Here you are.' She set the tray on the desk and he took a mouthful of the coffee and murmured appreciatively.

'I needed that. Thanks.' He chose one of the sandwiches as Georgia went to leave him. 'Georgia.'

She stopped and turned back to face him.

'Don't go.'

Her senses leapt at his husky tone. Or was she simply reading more into it than was really there—wishfully thinking?

'Stay and talk a while.' He motioned to the chair opposite the desk and Georgia slowly rejoined him, sitting quietly while he ate a couple of sandwiches and drained his coffee-cup.

Her hands fidgeted in her lap and she clasped them together to still their movements. Talk, he'd said. But what about? Surely he knew how difficult it was for them to discuss anything? At least, it was for her. Did he expect them to make light conversation? All very civilised. The weather, perhaps? What could she say?

You look tired. Let me soothe— For heaven's sake, what was wrong with her? She must be a masochist.

'Thanks for this, Georgia.' Jarrod broke the silence, indicating the empty tray. 'And for your help with everything the past few days.'

Georgia shrugged. 'I didn't really do much.'

'Yes, you did. My father...' he paused '...would have been pleased to know you were here.'

Georgia shifted uneasily in the chair. 'The service was very nice, wasn't it? Uncle Peter was well liked by everyone.'

'Yes,' Jarrod agreed flatly, and then leant back in his chair and sighed. 'You know, I don't think it's hit me yet that he's gone. Even being prepared for his death, as we all were— well, I still can't quite believe it. He was so...' He searched for the word. 'He had such a strong personality. When I was growing up, that's the one thing I remember about him—his strength of will.'

Jarrod stood up and paced over to the window.

'My father said that the accident Uncle Peter had all those years ago would have had anyone else in a wheelchair but that Uncle Peter's will-power got him walking again,' Georgia said softly. 'Dad said he was crushed under a falling crane. That must have been dreadful.'

'Yes. He had phenomenal will-power. Everyone admired him for that and yet—' Jarrod stopped, his back to her, and Georgia watched him hungrily.

Her eyes ran over him, over the hard contours of his body. He was a lot like his father, in colouring, in build, and he exuded that same strength.

'And yet?' she prompted him, feeling a flush wash her cheeks as she forcibly dragged her eyes from him.

'In the beginning I hated him.'

Georgia's breath caught sharply at the soft, flatly spoken words and Jarrod turned back to face her, resting his hips against the wide window-sill, folding his arms across his chest.

'But why?' she asked him.

'Because he showed me—' He gave an abrupt, negating movement of his head. 'No, that's not quite right. Because his appearance in my life made me realise the truth about my mother. Before Peter turned up I used to pretend.'

He ran a hand through his hair and Georgia drew a shaky breath, remembering Jarrod's reluctance over the years to discuss his mother and his life before he'd come to live with his natural father.

'Oh, I got over it. All this—' he indicated the room they were in '—was a far cry from the poky flat in suburban Perth where I used to live.'

'What happened?' Georgia questioned gently, and he pulled a face.

'The usual. Peter and my mother had a brief affair that resulted in me. For some reason my mother didn't want to tell him she was pregnant, and although Peter assured me he would have married my mother if he'd known we'll never know, will we? She—my mother—never wanted for male company during the years when I was growing up. Some of her "friends" were pretty good to me.'

He pushed himself away from the window-sill and paced restlessly again. 'But then, when she was between male friends, she discovered she had cancer, so she was forced to tell me about Peter Maclean.

'I think I went a little wild then. I'd always believed my father was dead and I refused to meet the man my mother now said was alive. Well, my mother died suddenly before we could resolve the issue and it was all taken out of my hands.

'A policeman rang Peter. He came over and we met for the first time. Not long after he brought me here.'

'Oh, Jarrod. I'm so sorry.' Georgia's heart ached for him. She couldn't recall Jarrod's first years with his father for she'd been quite young when Uncle Peter had adopted him. But he'd become great friends with Lockie.

Then, in his teens and early twenties, Jarrod had been away most of the time, studying or getting experience in other branches of his father's business. It was only later, when he'd returned for good, that they had finally come to love each other.

Or so she'd thought, Georgia reminded herself wearily.

'I suppose I must have been quite a handful at first,' Jarrod was continuing. 'I resented Peter. It seemed like my mother became ill and told me I had a father one minute, then she died and suddenly I was passed on to him. The kinder Peter was, the more I hated him.

'Strangely enough, at first I felt more akin to Isabel. It must have been difficult for her to have a surly adolescent thrust upon her but at least I knew where I stood with her. She was indifferent to me and didn't try to hide it.'

Georgia swallowed. When did that change? she wanted to ask him. When did the indifference develop into an affair?

Jarrod smiled crookedly. 'I guess Peter's perseverance wore me down, and I did come to respect him, until—' He stopped and his face grew even more drawn. He walked back to the desk and slowly sat down again. 'But no matter,' he added, as though he was unaware he was speaking.

'Do you have any other family? Back in Western Australia, I mean?' Georgia asked into the brooding silence that had claimed him.

'None I know of. My mother certainly never mentioned any.' His fingers moved a stack of papers on the desk and then he shook his head. 'What diabolical messes we mortals make of our lives,' he said with feeling.

Georgia could empathise with that. Her own life was a prime example of emotional chaos.

Jarrod let himself slump back in his chair and his eyes met Georgia's for one tortured, heart-stopping moment before his lashes fell to shield their expression.

'I have to go soon, Georgia.'

She blinked at him, not sure she'd heard the words. Then a terrible pain warred with the agony of recollection. Hadn't they played this scene before?

They were in the wrong place, she wanted to tell him. Shouldn't they be in the living room? And she'd tell him she never wanted to see him again. Yes, their life always seemed to be in replay mode. And for Georgia the pain wasn't any less this time around.

'When will you be leaving?' she heard herself ask with admirable self-control.

You've come a long way, Georgia Grayson, in these four years, she congratulated herself.

'Next week some time. As soon as I tie up everything here. I'll go back to the States.'

'What about the firm?'

'Maclean's? The set-up here can function without me. I can run it *in absentia*.'

She had to get up and go, Georgia told herself, before she broke down in front of him. Did she want to humiliate herself all over again?

No, she wouldn't allow herself to do that this time. She had some measure of pride now. But she couldn't stop the words that came out.

'The last time you left we said some hurtful things,' she said carefully, almost matter-of-factly, and she felt the immediate stillness in him. 'But I suppose we...' she paused '...I can blame that on the folly of youth.'

His eyes fell. 'The circumstances were different then.' He was equally unemotional.

'Yes, they were, weren't they?' She took a steadying breath. 'Will Aunt Isabel be staying here?'

'I have no idea. She may go down to the Gold Coast permanently.'

'I see.' Then Isabel wouldn't be going with him.

'There was never anything between Isabel and me,' he said quietly. 'I told you the truth about that. Look, Georgia,' he began, and shook his head slightly, 'about the last time. I know you thought at the time I was cruel, the way I told you how I felt, but there was more involved and I thought it was for the best, believe me.'

'Did you?' Georgia's mouth twisted in a sad, bitter little smile. 'Best for whom?' She sighed. 'Perhaps you were right. A sharp severance rather than a prolonged series of cuts, hmm?'

Jarrod's jaw was tight and his hands were out of sight, shoved into his pockets. He inclined his head. 'Something like that.'

On shaky legs Georgia forced herself to stand and he did too, the width of the desk between them.

'Well, it is the past, Jarrod,' she added flatly. 'I think we should leave it there, don't you?'

His gaze met hers and shied away.

She'd been content to do just that, she wanted to tell him, but then he'd come home and it had all flooded back over her.

'Can't we part as friends this time?' His words drew her eyes back to his face again.

'Friends?' Georgia repeated.

'We were that once.' He took a couple of steps around the desk, then he seemed to change his mind and stopped.

'And lovers.' Georgia held his gaze and she heard the soft hiss of his indrawn breath. 'I wonder how many old lovers remain friends? Not many, I should think. But I suppose it's the civilised thing to do.' She raised her eyebrows questioningly as he remained silent. 'Isn't it, Jarrod? Modern? Civilised?'

He turned slightly and leant against the desktop. 'As I said, we used to be friends.'

Georgia sighed. 'I think you know how impossible that would be. We could never be friends, Jarrod. At least, I can't. I'm sorry.'

'So am I.' His voice sounded thick, as though it was painful for him to speak.

'Well, I think I'll go and give Lockie and Andy a hand down at the house.'

Ask me not to go, something inside her begged him silently. Please, Jarrod, ask me to stay.

He slowly inclined his head and turned dismissively away.

'I'll probably see you later.' Georgia had to school herself to keep her voice steady, and as she left him she had to fight the urge to do exactly what she'd done four years ago. Run through the bush, blinded by tears, towards the sanctuary of home.

The pain choked her, held her in its anguishing grip. Four years on and it was just as severe.

When he'd come back into her life she'd hated him, living only for the moment when he would leave. Now she understood how closely aligned were the emotions of loving and hating. She could tell herself she still hated him but perversely she had to acknowledge that she loved him as much as she ever had. The hurt still ate at her but the love was burned indelibly into the deepest recesses of her soul. She'd never be free of it.

She made herself walk slowly, dry-eyed, towards home, and this time she made it without mishap. Without the devastating drama that had occurred four years ago.

A week later everything was falling back into place.

The conversation she had had with Jarrod in his father's study had seemed to act as a turning point for her. It had showed her that any small ray of hope she'd harboured after his kiss, his impassioned words in her dressing room was completely without substance. She must get her life in order. Alone.

The four years she'd spent drifting aimlessly must be recognised as her period of grieving. Now it had to end. She must draw it to a close herself. There was no future in the past. She had to reform her present and go on from there.

Surprisingly her realisation, her self-revelation, gave her strength.

Yes, everything was settling back to normal. Mandy had returned and was back singing with Country Blues. Their father would be home the next day to oversee the repairs to their house. Georgia could go back to concentrating on her studies and her job at the bookshop. And Jarrod was leaving to return to the States tomorrow afternoon, so there would be no constant expectation that he would keep appearing every time she turned around.

The past was behind her and her new life could begin. She should be happy, on top of the world. So why did she feel like crying?

Lethargically she climbed the stairs, grimacing at the sound of hammering coming from the back of the house. It was growing dark, so surely Lockie should be calling it a day?

Georgia had promised to pick up some fresh bread and milk for the boys on her way home from work and she was later than she would normally have been. In truth, she wasn't in any hurry to go back to the Maclean house to share a final meal with Jarrod. The hammering stopped, then started again, and now it seemed to have developed an echo.

Georgia sighed and stepped through the open front door. She was hot and tired from her walk from the bus stop and, juggling the bag of groceries, she shrugged off her jacket. A shower—she flexed her shoulder muscles—a long, cool shower was what she desperately needed, but that would have to wait until she went over to Jarrod's.

Her leg came up against a suitcase left inconveniently in the now dusk-lit hallway, and she grabbed for the wall to steady herself. The case was obviously full, for it hadn't budged when she'd tripped over it. She groaned and rubbed her bruised knee.

'That you, Georgia?' Andy appeared from the area of the damaged kitchen, switching on the temporary light that had been rigged up until the house could be rewired. He frowned as he took in the situation, the offending suitcase and Georgia on one leg inspecting her knee. 'Are you OK?'

'Almost.' Georgia pulled a face and grinned crookedly. 'If I'm not called upon to walk ever again.'

Andy reached out and took the bag of groceries from her. 'Come and shift your suitcase, young Morgan,' he called out. 'You left it in the middle of the hallway and Georgia fell over it.'

Morgan ambled out of the bedroom. 'Going blind now, Georgia?' she sniped as she slid the case sideways, closer to the wall.

'Just wasn't expecting to have to hurdle an obstacle in the hall, that's all.' Georgia's glance went from her sister's petulant face to Andy's disapproving one. Surely Morgan hadn't been arguing with Andy? Andy never quarrelled with anyone. Her heart sank. What was going on now?

The hammering stopped altogether and Georgia could hear the murmur of voices from the back of the house. Ken or Evan must be giving Lockie some help downstairs.

'Why the suitcase anyway?' Georgia absently asked her sister. 'I thought you were only staying with your friends until Dad comes home tomorrow.'

Morgan shrugged, her lips set defiantly. 'Because I'm giving you back your room, that's why.'

Georgia raised her eyebrows and her young sister lifted her chin.

'Steve's picking me up at seven-thirty,' she threw over her shoulder as she turned and sauntered into the living room.

Georgia glanced at Andy, who shook his head and shrugged before Georgia followed her sister, Andy close behind her.

'What are you talking about, Morgan?' Georgia asked.

'What does it sound like? I'm going back to the flat with Steve.'

'But you haven't even... When did you see Steve?'

'I've been seeing him for ages.'

Georgia hadn't even suspected that Morgan had had any contact with her boyfriend.

'While you've been becoming a star,' Morgan taunted.

'But—'

'Look, Georgia, we've talked it out, Steve and I, and I've decided to go back to him. Beginning, middle and end.'

'Morgan, I don't...' Georgia bit her lip, knowing that her open opposition would not go down well with her sister. 'Have you given this decision some thought?'

'What's to think about?' Morgan asked airily.

'Well, Steve did hit you, and it's not so very long since you were declaring you never wanted to see him again.'

'My sister of the long memory. I've got a long memory too, Georgia.' Morgan gave a laugh. 'Anyway, so I've had a change of heart.'

Georgia shook her head. 'I don't know what to say to you, Morgan,' she began tiredly.

'Probably what Lockie said, and what Mandy said before she left for work. How about "It's not the right thing to do"?' Morgan mocked. 'You said that the last time. "Living together—it's not right, Morgan." Well, what is, Georgia? Tell me that.'

'Morgan, for heaven's sake,' Andy interrupted, but the young girl ignored him.

'Well, what *is* right? Holding hands in the drive-in? Kissing goodnight on the front steps? Saving myself for Mr Right and marriage?' Morgan's laugh was harsh. 'Be thankful we're not doing it in the back seat of Steve's car like they did in the old days.'

'Morgan!' Lockie's voice came from behind Georgia's shocked stillness. 'That's quite enough.'

'Oh, shut up, Lockie. Don't try to tell me you're so lily-white, you and Mandy. But it has to be different for me, doesn't it? I'm too young, too immature to know what I want.'

'Morgan, please,' Georgia appealed to her sister. 'Let's not have another argument like the last one. Can't we talk about this calmly and rationally?'

'There's nothing to talk about, Georgia,' Morgan stated mutinously.

'Can't you see we're concerned about you?' Lockie asked, but Morgan laughed again.

'No doubt. But you don't have to worry about me. Any of you. I'm not stupid. I know where it's all at. And you can be sure I'm not going to go and get myself pregnant, like Georgia did.'

CHAPTER TWELVE

'PREGNANT? Georgia?' Andy croaked in astonished incredulity.

'How the hell—?' Lockie exclaimed at the same time.

'Yes, pregnant. And how the hell did I know?' Morgan finished. 'As I said, I'm not stupid. Even though I was only a kid I knew what was going on. You and Dad weren't so good at covering it up that night, were you, Lockie? You thought I was asleep but I wasn't. I overheard you talking.'

'Georgia?' Andy stepped forward, incongruously still holding the bag of groceries. 'What—? Is—?' He looked at Georgia's ashen face and a measure of doubt rendered him silent.

Georgia stood motionless. Stunned. Wondering if her hearing had deceived her. Perhaps it was her conscience, her guilty conscience, that had imagined those taunting, wounding words from her young sister. 'Pregnant, like Georgia…' Had Morgan really said that?

But Morgan didn't know. Only Georgia, her father, Lockie and their doctor had known about the child she'd carried. Jarrod's child. Oh, Jarrod. She almost groaned his name out loud.

'I even knew who the father was,' Morgan continued. 'You and Dad didn't, did you, Lockie? I knew where they met too.'

Georgia's head snapped up.

'They met down by the—'

Lockie grabbed Morgan's arm none too gently. 'You've said enough, Morgan. OK, so you know it all, but we don't

want to hear any of your salacious details, thanks all the same.'
He swore angrily. 'You're just a stupid little troublemaker.'
He gave her a shake.

Georgia moved then, putting a restraining hand on her
brother's arm. 'Lockie, please don't. Calm down.' She turned
to her sister, unaware of the pain clouding her eyes, but
Morgan recognised it and lost some of her insolent bravado.

Her gaze fell. 'It's true, isn't it, Georgia?' She looked de-
flated now, like someone who had dropped a huge bombshell
and suddenly wanted to draw it back.

'Morgan,' Georgia began softly, 'it was because of—' she
swallowed the lump in her throat '—because I know how
agonising one mistake can be, the whole thing, what I went
through…' She drew a breath, desperately wanting her sister
to understand but suspecting that she was making a king-sized
mess of the situation. 'That's why Lockie and I, and Dad, we
just try to protect you. We don't want to see you suffer the
way I did. Our advice was only given in your best interests,
because we love you.' Georgia's voice caught in her throat.

'Well, there's no need to protect me,' Morgan muttered, all
angry defiance gone. 'I'm taking that job at Jarrod's office.
I'm starting Monday and they're sending me on a computer
course at night school, so I'll be fine.'

Morgan met her sister's eyes and Georgia saw the regret
the young girl couldn't voice. Georgia nodded, turning
slightly, intending to make some explanation to Andy, who
still stood silently, quite obviously just a little embarrassed.

But Georgia's gaze went past him, her eyes widening in
horror.

Jarrod stood in the doorway, evidently having followed
Lockie upstairs, a witness to the dramatic little scene.

No one spoke.

Jarrod looked as though he'd aged ten years in those few
turmoil-filled moments. His cheekbones stood out against his
colourless face and he was drawn enough to look as though
he would fall down. But he didn't. He remained standing in

that same spot just inside the room, his eyes locked on Georgia in disbelief.

As she watched, held his haunted gaze, his disbelief turned to pain—a pain as great as any she'd suffered during that dreadful time after he'd left. His eyes were darkly tormented, reflecting the deepest agony.

'Georgia!' he rasped out. 'Oh, Georgia.'

Pain tore through her. For herself. For him. And she was galvanised into action. Before any of them could say a word she flew past Jarrod. Down the hall, almost coming to grief again over Morgan's suitcase. Down the wide front steps. Around the house to the back gate, fumbling as it caught again on rusting hinges, scrambling over it when it wouldn't budge. Along the path through the dry grass and bush, until she came gasping for breath to the bridge over the creek. The new solid footbridge.

If anyone called after her she didn't hear them, for blood pounded through her veins, echoing in her head like continuous claps of rolling thunder. She leant against the railings of the bridge, her hands massaging the stitch in her side as she drew in great gulps of air.

Gradually her breathing slowed and only then did she realise that tears were pouring down her cheeks. She blinked at the blurring dampness, wiping her wet face with her hand.

She looked down into the now dry, sandy watercourse and her heart lurched. She'd lain there until the early hours of the morning after she'd fled mindlessly from Jarrod that dreadful night. She'd not stopped in her headlong flight when she'd come to the creek, for she'd been so enveloped in her misery, in Jarrod's betrayal, not seeing or thinking past the awful truth—that Jarrod was having an affair with his stepmother, and that she never wanted to see him again.

She'd simply pounded straight over the old bridge, vibrating the rotting wood, her running weight being too much for its support to carry. The timber cracked beneath her, sending her screaming down onto the creek bed below.

The fall had knocked her out for some time—how long she didn't know—but she'd been lucky and had fallen with her face out of the shallow water or she would surely have drowned. Pain had racked her entire body when she had regained consciousness and, unable to move, she'd drifted in and out of delirium until her father and Lockie had found her there. She had broken her leg and lost her baby.

Georgia moaned softly. It had taken her so long even to begin to get over that loss—double-fold loss—of firstly Jarrod and then the baby. She'd clutched her pain to her and no one had known how she'd suffered inside herself. Perhaps her father or Lockie had suspected but after that night they'd never spoken of what had happened.

Geoff Grayson had asked who the father of her child was, of course, but she hadn't told him. And when he'd suggested it was Jarrod she'd denied it vehemently, saying it was someone else—someone she'd met secretly but wouldn't be seeing again. With hindsight, she felt she must have been a little demented at that moment, or perhaps her denial of him had been a subconscious act of vengeance. And, unbeknownst to Georgia, her brother had overheard her.

Her father had shaken his head in hurt and despair, barely able to comprehend the whole sordid mess. And *what* a sordid mess—

Georgia drew an alarmed breath, tensing at the sound behind her, and she swung jerkily about as the tall figure stepped onto the bridge. In the dimness of the heavy dusk she was unable to read his expression, but she caught the bright sparkle of the setting sun reflected in his eyes.

'It was my child, wasn't it?' he said flatly—a statement more than a question. 'Lockie said you told your father it was someone else's but I know it wasn't. The baby was mine. Why didn't you tell me, Georgia?'

'I intended to.' Her voice wavered feebly, her hands gripping the railing behind her to stop herself running into his arms. 'But then you...'

He was silent and then she heard him suddenly catch a sharp breath. 'That night, when you arrived... You were going to tell me then, weren't you? Oh, Georgia, I'm so sorry.' His tone revealed his distress, his regret. 'But that night...'

'It's the past, Jarrod, as you said before.'

'I don't know what to say, how to ask for your forgiveness.' His husky voice caught and he fought for a steadying breath. 'What...what happened? Lockie said—'

'I had a miscarriage when I fell.' She motioned to the creek bed below. 'When the bridge finally gave way. That's why your father had this new one built. He didn't know about the baby, only that I had fallen.'

Jarrod turned away and leant on the railings. 'If I'd known you were pregnant—' He stopped.

'You'd have stayed and married me,' Georgia finished wryly, and when he made no acquiescence her heart lurched in impossibly more pain.

His silence cut into her, baring her hurt like opening a throbbing wound.

'I couldn't have married you, Georgia,' he said softly. 'I should never have touched you.'

Georgia swallowed, trying to ease the tightness in her chest. 'It was a mutual thing, Jarrod, our...' she paused '...liaison. You didn't exactly seduce me.'

Jarrod swore beneath his breath. 'But I was old enough to know better, to be more careful. You were just a kid.'

'I was more than old enough. And I loved you, Jarrod,' she said, simply and honestly, and he straightened and turned back to face her.

'Don't you think I knew that?' he got out in a tortured voice. 'Is that my excuse?'

'I thought you loved me too.'

'I did.' The words were spoken so quietly that Georgia wasn't sure she'd heard them. 'God help me, I did love you, Georgia. I still do. But I can't.'

Georgia took a step towards him and his hands reached out

desperately for her, drew her to him, and she pressed her face against his chest. Beneath his cotton shirt she could hear the heady racing of his heart. His arms tightened urgently about her, but before she could slide her hands around him he had thrust her violently from him.

'Georgia, please. Don't. We can't—'

'Jarrod, why? What is it?'

'I can't tell you.' He wiped a shaking hand across his eyes.

'Why not? Jarrod!' She moved to close the space he'd put between them but his flatly spoken words froze her into immobility, turning her blood to ice.

'You're my sister, Georgia.'

CHAPTER THIRTEEN

How long they stood there, transfixed, Georgia couldn't have begun to guess, but eventually she gave a choked laugh. 'You have to be joking, Jarrod.'

'I wish I was. But it's the truth.'

'But that's… It's ridiculous. We'd have to have the same mother or fath—' Georgia stopped mid-syllable.

'Or father,' Jarrod finished flatly. 'Georgia, Peter Maclean was your father too.'

She began to shake her head.

'Remember the day we were both with him and he thought you were your mother. ''Darling Jenny,'' he called you. He was in love with your mother.'

'No, it's not true,' Georgia breathed. 'Who told you these lies?'

'Does that matter? And I'm afraid they're not lies.'

'They are,' Georgia repeated forcibly. 'Who told you, Jarrod? I have a right to know, don't I?'

He sighed and gave a faint nod of agreement. 'I guess you have. It was Isabel.'

'Aunt Isabel?' Georgia said in a daze. 'I can't— We can sort this out. I'll ask my father.'

'I've already asked mine,' he said flatly, and Georgia gazed at him in alarm. 'Don't you think I demanded the truth back then?'

'What did he say?'

'He denied it, of course. What else could he do? But he did

admit he'd always loved your mother. They were a couple until she met your father.'

'Your father wouldn't lie about this, Jarrod. And besides, what about Lockie? He's the image of my father. And why would my mother suddenly have...?' Georgia shook her head. 'No! I don't believe this, Jarrod. I won't.'

'What if it is true?' Jarrod asked softly.

'It's very convenient for Aunt Isabel that my mother isn't here to defend herself against these ludicrous accusations. Or your father.' Georgia's chin rose. 'Isabel has to be wrong. I don't care what you say, Jarrod, I'll never believe it. And I can't believe you can.'

She brushed past him for the second time and retraced her steps along the path to her home. But she walked this time, taut with shock, and Jarrod didn't follow her.

When she got back both Lockie and Andy exclaimed at her pale face, Lockie sitting her down and insisting on her having a glass of brandy, which nearly choked her.

Morgan had gone with Steve. Georgia wasn't to be upset about it, Lockie told her, and as to Georgia's secret—well, it was safe with them all. Obviously her brother must have made some explanation to Andy.

Georgia just shook her head. If only that had been the worst of it all.

Lockie had had a talk to the chastened Morgan after Jarrod had left and the young girl had broken down, telling him she'd been angry because they'd always treated her like a child, keeping her out of every decision or discussion, making her feel excluded, not part of the family. On reflection, Lockie admitted there might have been some truth in what Morgan had said and their efforts to shield their so much younger sister had only served to make her feel an outsider.

Georgia was far too numb even to begin to give the matter of Morgan any thought. Nor could she bring herself to mention to her brother Jarrod's horrible revelation. It was the only thing she could concentrate on, and it swirled around in her mind.

She didn't return to the Maclean house that night but slept on the couch in the living room of her own home. Peter Maclean her father? The thought went round and round inside her head throughout her sleepless night.

The next morning she rang the bookshop and told them she was unwell and wouldn't be coming to work. It wasn't strictly an untruth. Her stomach churned in unison with her harrowing thoughts.

She glanced at her watch for the hundredth time. Where was her father? Or rather the man she'd always looked upon as her father, and couldn't believe wasn't.

Yet when his car eventually turned into the driveway she found that her legs wouldn't hold her and she sank onto the lounge chair.

'Georgia?' Geoff Grayson stopped in surprise as he glanced into the living room. 'Georgia, what is it? Why aren't you at work? Are you ill?' He came to sit beside her, taking her cold hands in his, full of concern.

Georgia's eyes searched his lined face, seeking some substantiating resemblance to herself. But she was so like her mother, she knew. There was nothing to reassure her in the angular planes of his features, or in his colouring.

'I have to talk to you, Dad.' The form of address came naturally but she swallowed convulsively as she said it.

'Of course. What's the matter, love?' His fingers squeezed hers encouragingly.

'It's about… It's about you and Mum.' Georgia stopped. How could she ask her father this? But she had to. She had to know. 'Am I your daughter?'

It was out. She'd said it. But she couldn't meet her father's eyes.

Geoff Grayson laughed lightly. 'Well, that's the easiest question you've ever asked me. Of course you're my daughter. Don't you want to be?'

Georgia closed her eyes and thought she'd faint dead away.

Of course she wanted to be. But what if her father didn't know?

'Dad, are you…? Are you sure I was—well, is there any chance you're not my father?'

'Not your father? Georgia, this has gone far enough. Of course I'm sure I'm your father,' he said tersely, and stood up angrily. 'Your mother and I loved each other very much. There was never anyone else for either of us.'

Georgia burst into tears, sobbing brokenly.

Her father watched her for a moment and then sat down again beside her, his arms going around her. 'Don't you think it's time you told me what this is all about, love?' he asked gently.

'Oh, Dad, Jarrod said…he left because he thought he was… that Peter Maclean was my father too,' Georgia explained jerkily.

'Peter…? Georgia, what on earth are you talking about?' her father asked in astonishment.

'Jarrod said his father had always loved my mother and that…Aunt Isabel told him,' she finished as she dabbed at her eyes with the handkerchief her father passed her.

'Isabel told…? Georgia, look at me.' He tilted her chin until her eyes met his. 'If Isabel said that then she's mischief-making on a grand scale. Peter Maclean isn't your father and she knows it. It's completely impossible.'

'But how can you be sure?' Georgia persisted.

'Oh, I'm one hundred per cent sure, love.' Geoff Grayson shook his head sadly. 'It's an old story. You see, Peter and I both fell in love with your mother. He'd known her since childhood. Then he introduced us. Well, once I'd met Jenny there was only one woman for me. Peter felt the same about her but Jenny chose me.

'We were good friends, Peter and I, and he could have re-acted badly but he didn't. When he saw his case was hopeless, that Jenny had made her choice, he went over to the west coast for a few weeks to consult on a job over there. That was when he met Jarrod's mother. His affair with her must have been a rebound thing. Then, a few years later, before you were born and before he knew of Jarrod's existence, he flew back to Perth to open a new branch of Maclean's. He was only there for three months when he had that awful accident.'

'But—'

Geoff Grayson held up his hand. 'That accident he had nearly killed him, Georgia, and because of his massive injuries he couldn't have any children, so…' He shrugged.

Georgia's mind turned over the implication.

'He told me this himself, love,' her father continued. 'That's why it meant so much to him later, to learn he had a son.'

Georgia took a deep breath, relief flooding through her. 'If all this is true, Dad, why did Aunt Isabel tell Jarrod such blatant lies? What could she gain by it?'

'Isabel—well…' Her father shook his head again. 'I don't know. All this happened so many years ago. Peter, Isabel, Jenny and I, we went to dances, to picnics together. Your mother was so full of life, so loving. But Isabel was just the opposite. She's always been cool, reserved; you couldn't get close to her. Not even Jenny could. But to tell such lies to separate you and Jarrod!' He stood up angrily. 'I don't understand it. I'll go over and talk to her.'

'No, Dad. I'll go. I need to talk to Jarrod.' Feeling flowed back into Georgia's numb body and she was suddenly exhilarated. Aunt Isabel had lied. Jarrod still loved her. Everything would be all right.

'Make no mistake, Georgia, I will be speaking to Isabel. But in the meantime you can tell Jarrod he needn't take my word for all this. Peter's doctor will corroborate my story.'

'I love you, Dad. And even if you hadn't been—well, I'm glad you are.' Georgia blinked back a rush of relieved tears and gave her father a huge hug.

'I'm glad I am too.' He felt in his pocket and held out his keys with a crooked smile. 'Take my car, love. Now off you go.'

Georgia ran outside, feeling as though the weight of the world which had been pulling her down for four long years had finally lifted from her shoulders.

Isabel Maclean met Georgia at the door as she mounted the wide steps, and Georgia stood gazing levelly at the woman who was to blame for four wasted years.

'Why did you do it, Aunt Isabel?' she asked softly.

'Do what?' Isabel's fingers fiddled with her opal brooch. 'I'm sure I don't know what you mean.'

'Why did you tell Jarrod those lies about his father and my mother when you knew they couldn't possibly be true?'

'I said I don't—'

'Aunt Isabel, Uncle Peter was just that—my uncle by marriage. He wasn't my father and you know it. My father told me about Uncle Peter's accident.'

Isabel's finely coiffured head went up.

'You knew Uncle Peter couldn't have been my father and yet—' Georgia swallowed quickly. 'Do you know what you've done? The pain you've caused Jarrod? And me? Four whole years. I just don't understand why you did it.'

'Why?' Isabel grimaced. 'You could never begin to understand, Georgia.'

'I could try.'

'You're just like she was,' she said bitterly. 'Young. Attractive. Bubbling with personality. How could you understand what it's like to be the plain sister, the quiet, serious one?

'I lived in her shadow from the moment she was born. I could bear it until—' Isabel's lips twisted grimly. 'Jenny could have had any man she wanted. I couldn't. Why did she have to want Geoffrey Grayson?'

Georgia's eyes widened in surprise as she realised the truth. 'You were in love with my father?'

Isabel drew herself together. 'But of course he only had eyes for her.'

'You mean all this…? You told Jarrod those lies because…'

Georgia gazed at her aunt, really looking at her, and suddenly what she saw tempered her anger, leaving behind a reluctant compassion.

The older woman was tense, unbending, without humour. She had lost the man she loved nearly thirty years ago and she'd allowed it to embitter her so much that she'd maliciously tried to ruin the lives of two people who had had nothing to do with what had happened before they were born.

'Did it help assuage your need for vengeance?' she asked her aunt flatly.

'Nothing could do that,' Isabel said thickly, her eyes glittering angrily. 'Jarrod was the son I'd never have. And you—you're the image of your mother. Jenny was always the pretty one, the one everyone doted on—every *man* doted on. Peter wanted to marry her,' she added almost absently, her lips twisting bitterly. 'But she had to take Geoffrey from me.'

'Aunt Isabel—' Georgia stopped and shook her head. Was there any point in recriminations now? She could see now that her aunt had existed in an emotional void ever since, not letting anyone close to her. Not her husband. Not her stepson.

Georgia swallowed. Would she have turned out like her aunt? she asked herself. Cold, withdrawn, unforgiving? She shivered, suddenly cool in the warm, sunny morning. 'I want to see Jarrod,' she said levelly. 'Where is he?'

'He's gone. You're too late. He's left for the States.'

Georgia checked the time, agitation stirring in the pit of her stomach. 'His plane doesn't leave for three hours. He wouldn't have left yet.'

'He decided to catch an earlier flight. He's gone.'

'I don't believe you.' Georgia sidestepped her aunt and raced into the house, calling Jarrod's name, stopping when she reached his bedroom.

'Don't go in there, Georgia. How dare you break into my home?' Isabel's voice came from behind her. 'I told you, he's already left for the airport.'

Georgia paused and then swung open the door, catching her

breath when she saw Jarrod's luggage in a tidy pile by his bed.

'Where is he, Aunt Isabel?'

'I have no idea.' The older woman turned away and walked back along the passage, her back straight and uncompromising.

Georgia stood leaning on the door. Where could he be? If he'd been in the garden he'd have heard her calling him, surely? Had he gone to the office?

Then it came to her and she was running out of the house, through the scrubby trees towards the creek.

But he wasn't at the bridge, and for a moment she thought she'd been mistaken in thinking he'd come here one last time. Her step faltered and she went to turn back the way she'd come.

'Georgia.'

She glanced up and there he was, climbing to his feet from where he'd been sitting in the shade beneath the tree where they used to meet. He slid down the bank.

'I thought…' she began. 'I mean, I wanted to see you before you left…' Georgia's voice died on her and she swallowed. He was so undeniably attractive, standing with the high sun beating down on his head, burning gilded streaks in his dark hair. 'I had to tell you… Oh, Jarrod.'

It all poured out, the whole story, everything her father had told her. And then her conversation with Isabel.

'So, you see, it's not true, Jarrod!'

He looked dazed, then questioned her, made her go over it all again.

'Isabel admitted to me she'd lied, Jarrod, and as for your father's accident—Dad says everything can be verified by your father's doctor.' She watched the play of emotions pass across his face before a wondrous belief took over.

He slowly expelled the breath he'd been holding. 'When Isabel…' He shook his head. 'She was so convincing and it all seemed to fit, to explain so much. The relationship or lack

of it between Isabel and my father. The slightly strained atmosphere when your parents were there. I just couldn't doubt
what she told me.' He stiffened, his jaw tensing. 'How could
she do that to us? Why would she do it?' he exclaimed with
bitter disbelief. 'The wasted years. The baby. Dear God, I
could—'

'She's more to be pitied, Jarrod,' Georgia broke in. 'Her
life's empty. All she'll see before her is a replica of her past,
a chasm without any emotion. That's no sort of life.'

Jarrod put shaky hands on her shoulders, touching her
gently, reverently. 'How can you defend her after what she's
done, the pain she's caused?'

'Do you love me, Jarrod?' she asked him softly, her body
trembling beneath his touch.

'Desperately,' he replied with feeling. 'I've never stopped
loving you.'

'Then I can afford to be generous towards Isabel.'

'I don't think I can be as forgiving, love. And Isabel and I
will be having a talk later.' He drew her slowly into his arms,
kissing her tenderly, as though he thought she might disappear.
'Oh, Georgia. My darling Georgia. How I've yearned to hold
you again.'

Then they were clinging together, kissing, touching, mur-
muring in feverish abandon. When they finally broke apart
they were both breathless.

'I've needed that for so long,' Jarrod said huskily. 'These
weeks being back near you, thinking I dare not touch you,
failing more often than not. I thought I'd go crazy.' He took
her hand and drew her up the bank, under the sheltering shade
of the trees.

'Was it always this prickly?' he asked quizzically as they
sat down together, arms entwined, and Georgia giggled.

'What's a prickle or two?'

'Or three or four.' Jarrod's smile faded and he cupped her
cheek with his palm. 'Four years, Georgia. Four empty, wasted
years, when I was dying for you and sick to my stomach with

myself because I still wanted a woman I was sure was my half-sister.'

'Jarrod, don't.' Georgia closed her eyes and her tears squeezed from beneath her lashes.

'I know I hurt you, love, but I was raw with horror at what Isabel had told me. On top of her blatant obsessiveness over me when we were alone it was just about too much for me. And when you burst in on us I had no time to weigh up the situation.'

'I couldn't believe it when I saw you kissing her.'

Jarrod grimaced. 'I'm not proud of myself for that, but she—' He shook his head. 'When I came back from college and started spending all my time with you, that's when it started. The looks, the touching. I tried to ignore it, kept away from her as much as I could. I didn't know how to handle the situation. And then it blew up in my face.'

'She was in love with my father. She thought he'd betrayed her by marrying my mother.'

'I don't think Isabel knows what love is.' He sighed. 'All I knew at the time was that I couldn't bring myself to reveal Isabel's sordid story and that meant my only alternative was to leave. I knew you didn't believe me when I told you there was nothing between Isabel and me, but it was easier to go letting you think I was involved with Isabel than to tell you the truth. Even if it meant I left thinking you hated me. For going the way I did.' His thumb brushed the dampness from her cheeks.

'At first I was devastated, then when I lost the baby I was numb. I decided the best form of defence was to convince myself it had never happened. And when you came back, when I had to admit it *had* happened, I told myself I hated you, but—' Georgia's hand covered his '—I was fighting a losing battle. You're the other half of me, Jarrod, so I was hating myself. I was so confused—hating you, loving you. When you left I missed you so much.'

Jarrod held her to him, his hand smoothing back her hair.

'I don't know how I got through those years, Jarrod,' she whispered. 'I ate, I drank, I slept, I functioned like a robot. But I wasn't alive.'

'It was like that for me too. I was terrified to open each letter I got from home, yearning to hear some small thing about you but petrified to hear you were marrying someone else.'

'And I imagined you with all those gorgeous American girls.'

Jarrod gave a hoarse laugh. 'Remember suggesting I might have gone to bed with young Ginny?'

'I was so jealous—' Georgia began.

'There was no one, love. I've lived like a monk. There just wasn't anyone who came close to you.'

'Oh, Jarrod.' Georgia's heart soared. 'And there was no one else for me either.'

'Not even that red-bearded giant of a drummer?'

'Andy? No.' She shook her head. 'Never. We really are just friends.'

Jarrod pulled a self-derisive face. 'I came within centimetres of punching him out when he lifted you over the fence in that disgustingly blatant display of masculine muscle.'

Georgia grimaced. 'I think I subconsciously enjoyed using Andy to get to you that day.' Her eyes fell from his. 'You see, when you came home I thought I'd be able to deal with seeing you again. But one look and I fell harder and deeper than before. And I didn't want to; I fought the feeling so strongly. But you were still a part of me, Jarrod; you always were.'

'And I was so sure I would be able to keep away from you. I wanted you to hate me. It was safer, made it easier. But when you treated me like something that wasn't there I—well, I couldn't handle that, Georgia. I knew I'd never be free of you. And, even knowing what I did, thinking we were tied by blood, I didn't want to be free.'

'You did a really good job of not showing it,' Georgia teased him.

'Oh, I congratulated myself that I'd coped pretty well, until I saw you sing at the club. I was devoured by blazing jealousy, watching all those other guys watching you.' He groaned softly. 'I knew it would be like that.

'Which was the real reason why I tried to talk you out of singing with the band. It would have opened fresh fields for you. I knew I couldn't have you, Georgia, but I couldn't bear the thought of there being anyone else. Maybe Isabel and I have more in common than I thought.' His lips twisted wryly and then he held her gaze.

'I almost lost it that afternoon when I kissed you. And then you sang that song. It tore my heart out.'

Georgia buried her face in his shirt. 'And I was so horrible to you afterwards in the dressing room. I goaded you. I couldn't seem to help myself, stop myself hitting out at you.'

'I deserved it. And more.' He paused. 'Did you really write that song the night after we first made love?'

Georgia nodded. 'It was so wonderful, I… The song wrote itself. I never had any intention of singing it to anyone but you back then, but Lockie found it and you were so against anything to do with my part in Country Blues…' She shrugged. 'I was so mixed-up and unhappy.'

'Well, I couldn't begin to describe what seeing you, hearing you sing it did to me.' He sighed. 'That night I nearly told you why I'd left. And then again in the study the day after my father's funeral.'

They gazed at each other in silence for long moments and Georgia felt her heart shift in her chest. Her heartbeats fluttered, soaring like a bird on ecstatic wings. For the first time in four years she felt alive, really alive, a living, breathing human being.

'Lockie will be making the record,' Georgia told him.

'It's a fantastic song but I'm selfish enough to not want you to make it public.' He ran his finger gently along the line of her jaw. 'Are you sorry Mandy will be singing the song in your place?'

Georgia shook her head. 'Most definitely not. After the first time I knew I could never sing it again. And as to being part of Country Blues, I've never wanted that kind of life.'

He held her in the circle of his arms and she sighed tiredly. 'I'm so glad it's all over—all the pain, the heartache.'

'Georgia, about the baby. I feel so bad, so responsible. If I hadn't caused you to run off into the night—'

'Aunt Isabel was the one who set the wheels in motion,' she reminded him.

'But—'

Georgia put her finger on his lips. 'Don't, Jarrod. We can't dwell on what's past. I'll never forget the joy I felt knowing I was pregnant, but losing the baby—well, it's something that happened that we can't change. We have to put it behind us, start from now. Besides—' her smile was bitter-sweet '—there can be other babies. The doctor told me.' She let her fingertips slide along the line of his jaw and back to trace the outline of his lips. 'So…'

'So?' he queried huskily, taking her finger in his mouth, his eyes glowing with the passion she remembered so well, had thought never to see again.

'So, we can do it again. That is, if you remember how we managed it last time.' Georgia gazed up at him with widened eyes and he laughed throatily.

'I might need you to jog my memory. But perhaps we should make a start by feeling our way,' he added, his fingers caressing her ear lobe, moving down from her shoulder, running lightly over her breast where it swelled beneath her light blouse.

'Retrace our steps?' Georgia raised one eyebrow and began to unbutton his shirt, slipping her fingers inside to feel the firm flesh of his flat midriff.

'And practise.' Jarrod's hands reached her waist, lifted her blouse over her head, dropping it onto the ground. 'Practice is most important.'

'Most,' Georgia agreed, sliding his shirt off his shoulders, gliding her hands over those tanned, familiar contours. 'Practice makes perfect, I've heard.'

'Could it be more perfect, love?' he asked thickly.

'We'll have to put it to the test, don't you think?' Georgia's body was on fire as she fought to maintain her light tone, in keeping with the superficial teasing that cloaked the arousing sensuousness of their caressing hands.

'Then perhaps we should start swapping clinches for clichés,' Jarrod smirked, his eyes alight, bright burning blue.

'Actions for adages,' Georgia quipped back as she unbuckled his belt. All the while they touched, fingers and lips setting each other aflame.

'It's going to be difficult, Georgia,' Jarrod murmured with mock uncertainty.

'I don't think so.'

'It has been four years,' he reminded her as he lifted himself, helping her slip off his jeans.

'I have every faith in your photographic memory.'

'You do?'

'Absolutely.'

'Then I think we should put such faith to the test, hmm?' He dispensed with the rest of her clothes.

They were both naked now, drinking in the smoothness of each other, and the years between began to slip away.

'I do believe it is just like riding a bicycle—you never forget.' Jarrod's ragged breath caressed her ear lobe, sending spirals of desire surging through her.

'Jarrod?' Something was teasing the back of Georgia's mind.

'Mmm.' His lips traced the line of her jaw.

'Talking of bicycles, what about your plane?'

'What plane?' He was gently kissing the sensitive spot where her pulse beat in her neck.

'The one you were leaving on.'

'I hear it's been grounded.'

'Grounded?'

'Snow.'

'Snow? In Brisbane in summer?'

'Mmm.'

'Oh.' Georgia made a tiny moaning sound deep in her throat as his lips nudged the soft skin beneath her breast, gradually climbing upwards until they found one taut rosy peak. 'If you say so, Jarrod,' she breathed brokenly.

'I most definitely do say so, Georgia Grayson. I have this feeling in my bones.'

'In your bones?' Georgia's fingers followed the slope of his firm, flat stomach, encircling the indentation of his navel.

'Mmm,' he murmured responsively. 'Make that a feeling in every inch of me.'

'Every delicious inch of you.' Georgia gave a sensuous chuckle and slid her body down the length of his, and he caught his breath.

'Oh, Jarrod, touch me,' she whispered softly, and the warm, light breeze sighed in the dry leaves overhead.

The world's bestselling romance series.

HARLEQUIN®
Presents~

Seduction and Passion Guaranteed!

Introducing Jane Porter's exciting new series

**The Galván men: proud Argentine aristocrats...
who've chosen American rebels as their brides!**

IN DANTE'S DEBT
Harlequin Presents #2298

Count Dante Galván was ruthless—and though it broke Daisy's
heart she had no alternative but to hand over control of her family's
stud farm to him. She was in Dante's debt up to her ears! Daisy
knew she was far too ordinary ever to become the count's wife—
but could she resist his demands that she repay her dues in his bed?

On sale January 2003

LAZARO'S REVENGE
Harlequin Presents #2304

Lazaro Herrera has vowed revenge on Dante, his half brother, who
refuses to acknowledge his existence. When Dante's sister-in-law
Zoe arrives in Argentina, it seems the perfect opportunity. But
the clash of Zoe's blond and blue-eyed beauty with his own
smoldering dark looks creates a sexual force so strong that
Lazaro's plan begins to fall apart....

On sale February 2003

**Pick up a Harlequin Presents® novel and you will enter
a world of spine-tingling passion and
provocative, tantalizing romance!**

Available wherever Harlequin books are sold.

HARLEQUIN®
Makes any time special ®

Visit us at www.eHarlequin.com

HPGALVAN

International bestselling author

SANDRA MARTON

invites you to attend the

WEDDING *of the* YEAR

Glitz and glamour prevail in this volume
containing a trio of stories in which
three couples meet at a
high society wedding—and
soon find themselves
walking down the aisle!

Look for it in November 2002.

$ Saving Money $ Has Never Been This Easy!

Just fill out and send in this form from any October, November and December 2002 books and we will send you a coupon booklet worth a total savings of $20.00 off future purchases of Harlequin and Silhouette books in 2003.

Yes! It's that easy!

I accept your incredible offer!
Please send me a coupon booklet:

_____
Name (PLEASE PRINT)

_____
Address   Apt. #

_____
City   State/Prov.   Zip/Postal Code

In a typical month, how many
Harlequin and Silhouette novels do you read?

❏ 0-2   ❏ 3+

097KJKDNC7   097KJKDNDP

Please send this form to:
In the U.S.: Harlequin Books, P.O. Box 9071, Buffalo, NY 14269-9071
In Canada: Harlequin Books, P.O. Box 609, Fort Erie, Ontario L2A 5X3

Allow 4-6 weeks for delivery. Limit one coupon booklet per household. Must be postmarked no later than January 15, 2003.

HARLEQUIN®
Makes any time special ®

Silhouette®
Where love comes alive™